HOLBROOK

A LIZARD'S TALE

HOLBROOK

A LIZARD'S TALE

★

BY
Bonny Becker

ILLUSTRATED BY
Abby Carter

CLARION BOOKS ★ NEW YORK

Clarion Books
a Houghton Mifflin Company imprint
215 Park Avenue South, New York, NY 10003
Copyright © 2006 by Bonny Becker
Illustrations © 2006 by Abby Carter

The illustrations were executed in black colored pencil and wash.
The text was set in 13-point Bembo.

www.clarionbooks.com

Printed in the U.S.A.

Library of Congress Cataloging-in-Publication Data
Becker, Bonny.
Holbrook: a lizard's tale / by Bonny Becker ; illustrated by Abby Carter.
p. cm.
Summary: Holbrook the lizard has an artist's soul, but when his paintings are
ridiculed by the owls, geckos, and other creatures in his desert town, he decides to
seek his fortune in the big city, unaware of the dangers of urban life.
ISBN-13: 978-0-618-71458-2
ISBN-10: 0-618-71458-8
[1. Lizards—Fiction. 2. Artists—Fiction. 3. City and town life—Fiction.]
I. Carter, Abby, ill. II. Title.
PZ7.B3814Ho 2006
[Fic]—dc22
2006003962

MP 10 9 8 7 6 5 4 3 2 1

★

For Katie and Nicki,
with all my love
—B. B.

★

To Carrie
—A. C.

★

You are kind to painters and I tell you the more I think, the more I feel that there is nothing more truly artistic than to love people.

—Vincent Van Gogh, in a letter to his brother

For inspiration and help in writing *Holbrook: A Lizard's Tale*, thank you so much to the following people: First of all, to Michael Kreamer, San Francisco artist and original inspiration for Holbrook. To Doug Shaeffer who shared with me his knowledge of opera. To the many friends and fellow writers who looked through my many, many drafts and kept encouraging me along the way, including Susan Taylor Brown, Kathryn Galbraith, Mari Gower, Sylvie Hassock, Eve Kiehm, Kirby Larson, Susan O'Keefe, Ellie Matthews, David Patneaude, Edith Rohde, Laura Purdie Salas, and Judith van Praag. Special thanks, too, to my agent, Tracey Adams, who sent Holbrook out into the world for me, and to Clarion editor Jennifer Greene, who not only "got" Holbrook, but who was instrumental in shaping the final story. And as always—to Doug.

HOLBROOK

A LIZARD'S TALE

1

Beneath the high desert sky, under stars glittering and grand, a young lizard trudged toward a dusty, worn-down building. The sand made a firm *skrinch, skrinch* under his long toes. His fingers curved around a painting that was carefully covered with a cloth.

Off in the distance, a great horned owl hooted softly, "Whoooo's awake?" Then the owl answered himself, as owls like to do, "Me, too. Me, too."

The lizard glanced down at his painting. Tonight, Holbrook thought, he would show the other animals of Rattler's Bend that he was an artist. A real artist. Tonight they would finally see how important and special he was . . . wasn't he?

Holbrook swallowed nervously and looked up. The sky soared above him. The last little stars hanging there seemed so far away. He had read somewhere that the light from some of them had taken a million years to reach the Great Desert. Holbrook supposed he was just the tiniest speck standing there. But inside he felt something so big, he thought he might burst with it.

The big thing inside made him want to paint. He wasn't sure why. It just seemed there were important things to say and do in the world. Holbrook often wondered if any of the other desert animals felt that way, too. But he didn't suppose so.

None of them read books the way he did. Holbrook had three books tucked back in a special hole in his burrow. He had read them over and over. From them he had learned of grand things: of giant cities and tall buildings that almost touched the sky, of animals who did all kinds of exciting things, even some who were artists, as he wanted to be.

Holbrook tightened his grip on his painting and hurried on to Irving's General Store and Desert Diner. Irving had invited Holbrook to show his painting there. Right now, near dawn, the restaurant would be full of desert creatures eating breakfast after a long night harvesting salt at the Great Salt Flats.

Most everyone in Rattler's Bend worked at the flats—the bed of an ancient dried-up sea. Nobody in Rattler's Bend had ever been anything like an artist. That's why Irving thought Holbrook should show the others. "Let folks see what you're up to," the iguana had said. "You can't play forever, you know."

"I'm not playing!" Holbrook had protested.

Playing wasn't a thing you did for long in Rattler's Bend. Every creature got its season of youth—folks would give you that—but then it was time to grow up and figure out your place in the world.

Holbrook paused outside Irving's. Inside, he could hear the clatter of dishes but no talk. The hard-working animals were tired by dawn.

Holbrook could feel his long pale throat pulse as it did when he was scared or excited. He wasn't sure which he felt.

He squared his tiny shoulders and pushed open the door.

2

Inside the diner, lizards sat hunched over their flapjacks, staring at their plates and chewing slowly. Holbrook suddenly wanted to go home. He'd barely told anyone about his dream of being an artist. And, even worse, he knew that his paintings were . . . well, *different*. Even in his books, Holbrook had never seen paintings like his. A tiny voice inside his head said, "Squiggles."

And he glanced at Jagger, the horned lizard, who, as usual, sat alone in a corner.

Just then Irving limped up. "You brung it?" he asked.

Holbrook nodded.

"All righty, then." The iguana flapped a soiled dishtowel for attention. "Holbrook's got something to show us."

All around the diner, knives and forks stopped scraping. Crink and Crank, the twin geckos, turned their soft oversized heads in Holbrook's direction.

The red-spotted toad's bulgy eyes bulged even more.

Jagger looked up, then shoved his chair around.

Holbrook flushed. He'd never shown his paintings to anyone—except once Jagger had sneaked up on him while he painted behind the big rocks. Jagger had stared, then sneered. That's when he'd said, "Squiggles," and scurried away.

Jagger had teased him about it ever since.

Holbrook cleared his throat. Earlier, he'd thought of a speech. "I know that folks have wondered what I've been up to and when I'll get to work," he said.

Several animals nodded.

"And I have been working. Hard."

The animals looked pleased.

"The thing is, well, I—I intend to be an artist." Holbrook stammered over this last part.

"What?" said the red-spotted toad. "What'd he say?"

"Artist. He wants to be an artist," said Irving.

The animals looked baffled.

"You know—paint pretty pictures," Irving offered. He waved a forepaw at a picture of a cactus on a calendar on the wall.

The animals still looked confused.

"Show 'em," Irving said.

Holbrook took a deep breath, then lifted the cloth from his painting.

It was a picture of a starry sky, like the sky he had looked up at earlier—only not exactly. It was made of curls of velvety blue and bursts of star-glow white that swirled and shimmered all over the canvas.

Holbrook supposed his painting didn't look like any *real* sky, not like a photograph, but even so he was sure it was the best painting he had ever done. He had worked harder on it than on any painting ever before, and when he looked at it, he could feel how important the stars were. It made him feel important, too.

A large brown chuckwalla coughed. Then with an embarrassed downward glance, he went back to eating his flat cakes.

"Squiggles," muttered Jagger.

Holbrook suddenly felt stiff and burning hot.

"Well, now," said Irving, a worried frown on his wrinkled snout. "That's right, ur, right interesting. What's it called?"

Holbrook's tongue felt stiff, too, but he managed to scrape out, "I call it *Starry Sky*."

"*Starry Sky*?" said the red-spotted toad. "Where're the stars? Where's the sky?"

"Squiggles," Jagger said a little louder.

Crink and Crank giggled.

"They're not squiggles," cried Holbrook.

His throat was beating so hard, it hurt.

He knew his pictures didn't look exactly real. Not like a real creosote bush or a real red-tailed hawk. But he wasn't trying to do that. He had been able to draw how things really looked practically since he was hatched, scratching pictures in the dirt with a twig. He wasn't trying to show how things *looked;* he was trying to show how they *felt.*

"They're not squiggles," he said again. "They're feelings. They make you feel things."

"Well, when I look at that," drawled the chuckwalla, "I feel kind of sorry for you."

Irving stared at the floor. Crink and Crank snorted with laughter. Holbrook felt himself shaking like a cottonwood leaf. Didn't *anyone* think it was good?

"Time to put away the finger painting, son," said the chuckwalla, suddenly shoving back his chair and standing.

The other animals stretched and stood, too. It was time for bed. They shuffled past Holbrook and out the door, not looking at him. Jagger stared at *Starry Sky* for a whole minute, as if he couldn't believe how bad it was, then scuttled out behind the other lizards.

"Sorry, Holbrook," said Irving, twisting his dishtowel in his hands. The old iguana had a worried look on his snout. "Say, would you like a pickled egg?" He waved toward a jar of greenish white blobs on the counter. "You can have one free."

Holbrook just kept staring at his painting. Didn't anyone see how big the sky was and how the stars shimmered—not like real stars, maybe, but like stars in a dream?

"Tell you what," said Irving. "You can come work regular here. I could use a full-time dishwasher, and, well, there's sweeping, too."

Holbrook didn't answer. He couldn't answer. The lump in his throat was too big. He wrapped up *Starry Sky* and hurried away.

3

Holbrook stared at the gray dishwater in the sink at the Desert Diner and swallowed back a sigh.

It was two days since he had shown everyone *Starry Sky*. He'd hidden in his burrow all the first day, but finally he'd gone to Irving's and said it was time he got a job. A real job. And then he'd set to work sweeping and carrying boxes of goods and washing dishes.

"Package came for you," said Irving, holding up a fat parcel wrapped in brown paper.

It was art supplies. Holbrook had ordered them two weeks earlier from the big general catalog in Irving's store. But it didn't matter now.

He scrubbed hard at a scratched drinking glass.

"Well, I'll just set this right here," said Irving, shoving the parcel toward Holbrook. He gave Holbrook a clumsy sort of pat and limped through the swinging kitchen doors back into the diner.

Holbrook tried not to look at the package. He

tried not to think about the colors he had ordered.

Burnt sienna. Viridian. Cobalt blue. Colors that became feelings.

He set down the chipped plate he should have been washing and stared out the window. The stars were faint smudges through the dirty glass.

Holbrook ignored the package all his shift, but as he headed out the door after work, Irving pushed it into his hands.

"Take it," he ordered.

Holbrook hesitated, then grabbed it.

He thought he would drop it by the big creosote bush, then he thought he would drop it behind the rocks, then he figured he'd heave it into the gully, and then he was at his burrow. The wind had picked up, and he ducked inside just ahead of a sandstorm.

Holbrook set the package by his doorway. He didn't know what to do. He thought he could squish down the big thing inside him until he didn't feel it anymore. But if he went to the back of his burrow, he would see his books. If he went to the front of his burrow, he would see the package. Stacked against the sides of his burrow were all his old paintings. His dream was everywhere.

He looked at the package; he couldn't help wondering if they'd sent the special brush he ordered.

Holbrook tugged at the string around the package and spread open the brown paper with a sharp crackle.

Inside were his paints and a new brush soft as a cactus flower and a yellow notice.

It read:

ATTENTION, ALL ARTISTS.

COME ONE, COME ALL, AS WE DISCOVER
THE GREATEST ANIMAL ARTISTS
IN THE WORLD
AT GOLDEN CITY'S
ARTISTE EXHIBITION EXTRAORDINAIRE.

SINGERS, DANCERS, POETS, PAINTERS—
ALL THE GREAT ARTISTS WILL BE THERE.
AND HOPEFUL NEWCOMERS, TOO.

ALL ARE WELCOME!

WE WILL PICK THE GREATEST AMONG THEM
FOR A GRAND WORLD TOUR.

COULD IT BE YOU?!

Holbrook read it. He put it back in the package. He touched the fat white tubes of paint. He closed up the package.

He sat near his doorway, leaning against the wall, his knees bent high and his tail wrapped over his shoulder. He stared out at the blowing sand. Dark and swirling, it scoured the land.

Holbrook opened the package, took out the notice again and stared at it for a long time.

4

Holbrook pulled *Starry Sky* from its wooden stretcher bars. He gently rolled the painted canvas up and tucked it inside his backpack.

He had thought about it for a long time, and he had decided: He would go to Golden City. Maybe he could show his painting in the Exhibition! Maybe. But even more important, maybe there someone would understand about showing how things felt. Maybe there they wouldn't look down at the floor or talk about squiggles.

He hoisted the pack on his back. He took one last look around his home. He thought of all the nights he'd spent reading his books and dreaming of grand things by the golden light of his candle.

But this wasn't a story in a book. Would he find something grand? Something big and wonderful? Well, if he didn't, he supposed he'd just never come back and no one would ever know.

He threw his favorite yellow scarf around his neck, then quickly stepped out the door.

He stopped by Irving's to say goodbye. "I'm off to Golden City," he announced.

Irving looked as astonished as Holbrook had hoped he would. "Whatever for?" asked the iguana.

"I'm going to enter my painting in a contest."

"Hmm," Irving got out his dust rag and started pushing the remains of the sandstorm around. The sand never went far, and it always came back.

Holbrook noticed the red-spotted toad listening in from the back of the store. She quickly turned and pretended to be examining a cactus-spine comb. "Only, I've, uh, got a question," said Holbrook, glaring at the toad and trying to sound as if he wasn't nervous. "How far is Golden City?"

"'bout three hundred miles," said Irving. He had gone all the way to Near Forks once in his youth and knew about the world beyond.

Three hundred miles! Holbrook couldn't believe it. It took him a long time to walk just one mile. It would take him forever to get to Golden City. If he didn't die first. There were probably a lot of ways a small lizard could get hurt in three hundred miles. He'd never make it.

"There's always the bus," said Irving, as if reading Holbrook's mind.

Holbrook had never taken the bus. He'd never been farther from Rattler's Bend than he could walk in a few hours.

"Does it cost a lot of money?" said Holbrook.

"Not much," said Irving. "Five dollars or so."

Holbrook had five dollars tucked in the corner of his backpack, but it was all the money he had.

"Do you think I should go?" he asked.

"It's a mighty big world out there," Irving said, taking another swipe at the sand.

Holbrook suddenly remembered that Irving never would give you an answer straight. He just said things that could mean anything. If what you did worked out, he acted as if that's what he had told you. If it didn't, he acted as if he'd tried to warn you.

Holbrook swallowed. "I'll do it," he said quickly, before he could take it back.

"Well . . . if you say so," said Irving. He turned and grabbed something out of the cooler behind him. "Here, take this." He thrust a thick sandwich wrapped in wax paper at Holbrook. "It's a long ride."

Together, they walked to the road—a long lonely gray ribbon that ran through the desert. The animals of Rattler's Bend didn't usually have much to do with it.

By the road was a pullout where the bus stopped if someone was waiting. The bus didn't stop often.

"Now, listen up, Holbrook," said Irving. "I want you to know that you're always welcome back here. The city animals, well, they might not understand, see. Don't let it get you down, all right?"

Holbrook didn't want to think about that. In the city, the animals *would* see. They just had to. There the creatures were much finer than the ones here. He'd read about them in his books.

But he thanked Irving for the advice.

Before long, he noticed a wisp of dust far down the road, and then he heard the rattle of an engine. An old silvery bus came up over the rise and lurched toward them. Irving raised his arm, and the bus squealed to a halt. The door opened with a wheeze.

Holbrook stared for a moment at the wide steps rising into the darkness of the bus. He hesitated.

Just then, to his surprise, Jagger, the horned lizard, darted up to him.

"I hear you're leaving," said Jagger.

Holbrook nodded.

"You taking that squiggly painting?"

"It's not squiggles!" cried Holbrook.

"You coming or not?" croaked the bus driver, a large desert toad.

Holbrook glanced again at the bus steps, then back at the desert.

"Here," said Jagger. "This is yours." He thrust a small artist's paintbrush at Holbrook.

Holbrook recognized it. He'd lost it several months before and couldn't figure out where it had gone. Jagger probably thought it was funny to take his art stuff. Now that he thought about it, he was missing a bunch of things!

But before he could say anything, Jagger scurried off, his flat brown body disappearing quickly against the desert sand.

"Jagger stole my paint—" Holbrook began.

But the bus driver had started to close the door, and Irving yelled, "Go! Now!"

It was the most direct thing Irving had ever said, and Holbrook turned and leapt through the closing door, just in time. He scrambled to his feet and handed the driver a crumpled five-dollar bill. All the money he had.

"Golden City, please," Holbrook said.

He found a seat in the back, and the bus pulled away with a belch of oily smoke. Holbrook raised a hand to wave goodbye, but he wasn't sure Irving could see him through the dirty window.

The bus picked up speed, and the desert turned into a blur, like one of Holbrook's paintings. He noticed he still held the paintbrush Jagger had given him—or rather, had given back to him. He imagined Jagger waving it around and making fun of him in front of the other animals.

Squiggles.

What if the city animals thought his painting was squiggles, too? What if they laughed, too? What if they *didn't* see? What if it wasn't any different, after all?

5

It was late afternoon when the bus rattled over a tall, soaring bridge. Holbrook slid open his window and pressed his snout as far out as he dared. Gone were the scrubby brown hills of the desert. Against the skyline rose spires and spikes of stone and a thousand thousand windows glinting in the lowering sun. Golden City. The signs said so. Holbrook's heart said so. The blue waves of a bay sparkled below; there was the smell of salt water in the air and a hum, constant and unending. It seemed to say to Holbrook, "The city. The city. All dreams come true in the city."

At the end of the bridge, the bus swooped down onto the busy streets. Holbrook stared and stared. He could barely take in building after building rushing by, and all the animals—dogs and squirrels, pigeons and rabbits! And horns blowing, tires squealing, and walk signs blinking on and off.

The bus pulled into a station amid the tall buildings of downtown.

Holbrook grabbed his backpack and followed an excited desert sparrow out of the bus and onto the street outside the station.

But then he stood there, not sure what to do next.

"Excuse me," he asked a passing crow. "Can you tell me where the Artiste Exhibition is?"

"Not interested," snapped the crow.

"Excuse me," Hobrook tried asking a plump hamster, but the hamster brushed past with a surly "Get lost!"

A cat stared at Holbrook from the shadows of a nearby alley, and Holbrook decided he'd better get moving. He scurried down the street, keeping close to the buildings and away from the hurrying creatures of the city. Never had he seen so many different animals.

Sleek city-fed squirrels passed by, filling the air with chatter and argument. A miniature poodle with a diamond necklace smiled at him before she whisked into a low doorway. He'd never seen a poodle except in his books. He'd never seen almost everything!

Everywhere were pigeons. They cooed with the happenings of the city. They murmured from park bench to front stoop to windowsill. The cooing spread out like a wave and back in again, a ceaseless tide of gossip and news.

And it said, "Things are happening in the city. The city. The city. All dreams come true in the city!"

Then Holbrook saw a sign taped onto a telephone pole. It read:

GOLDEN CITY'S
ARTISTE EXHIBITION EXTRAORDINAIRE

An arrow pointed up the hill.

Holbrook's heart beat faster. There it was! The Exhibition. All the greatest artists in the world would be there . . . and maybe one would look at his painting!

He began to run and didn't notice the light changing up ahead. He hurried into the street. Cars hurtled toward him. *Honk! Screech!*

Holbrook dove for the sidewalk. Something hit him with a heavy thump. Up he flew, the backpack torn from his grip. He tumbled over and over, landing so hard that for a moment he couldn't breathe. Things went black.

Then slowly he became aware of three scruffy pigeons staring down at him. The pigeon on the left had only one eye. Suddenly, he pecked at Holbrook's tail.

"Ouch!" Holbrook cried.

"It's alive," announced the middle pigeon, sounding disappointed.

"What is it?" rasped the third pigeon, whose skin showed scabby pink through its sparse feathers.

Lone Eye circled him, turning his head this way and that to get a good look.

"It might be a snake with legs," Lone Eye said.

"Or a frog with a tail," suggested the middle pigeon, hopping closer. Holbrook saw that he only had one leg.

"Let's see if he dies," said the scabby one. "And then we can eat him."

The other two bobbed their heads eagerly.

Holbrook quickly sat up. "I'm Holbrook," he said. "I am not a snake or a frog. I am a lesser earless lizard of the Great Desert."

The pigeons were still staring eagerly.

"And I'm not edible!" said Holbrook, standing all the way up.

"Oh." The scabby pigeon eyed him with disappointment.

"Can you spare a crumb?" asked One Leg, hobbling closer.

Holbrook backed away and shook his head. Suddenly, he remembered his pack. He still had half of the sandwich Irving gave him in there, but more importantly, *Starry Sky* was in it!

Holbrook quickly looked around.

"Did anyone see where my pack went?"

The pigeons acted as if they hadn't heard him.

"Crumbs for the poor?" they cooed at the passing animals, although no one paid any attention. Then Holbrook saw the scabby pigeon glance toward a big cement planter with a dead bush in it.

He hurried over. There was his pack, behind the planter. He opened it and checked on *Starry Sky*. The painting was safe.

The pigeons peered over his shoulder with undisguised curiosity. "I see you have some bread in there," said Lone Eye.

Holbrook didn't answer but quickly shoved Irving's sandwich back deep into his pack. He would need it himself.

"I'm here for the Artiste Exhibition Extraordinaire," he said. "The big Exhibition to find the greatest artists in the world? Do you know where it is?"

One Leg glanced at his friends. "Anyone know what he's talking about?"

"Noooo, noooo," murmured the others, turning away.

But again Scabs couldn't help glancing to her side. Holbrook followed her glance to an Exhibition poster with an arrow pointing to the right.

He quickly shouldered his pack and headed off in the direction of the arrow.

"Crumbs? Crumbs for the poor?" the pigeons murmured behind him.

The Exhibition Hall was bigger than Holbrook expected. Wide steps led up to a huge double doorway flanked by columns of stone. Holbrook tugged on one of doors. It was so heavy, he had to use both forepaws to pull it open. He slipped inside just before it thudded shut behind him.

The sound echoed through a vaulted chamber of cold marble. In the center was a desk with a rat sitting behind it.

Holbrook crossed the empty chamber and approached the rat, who stared at him with hard gray eyes.

"I'm here for the Exhibition," Holbrook said, hoping he was in the right place.

"Application?" said the rat holding out a paw.

"Application?"

"And come back next Tuesday."

"I—I don't have an application," said Holbrook.

The rat, sighing as if the weight of the world were

upon him, pulled a sheet of paper from his desk. "Fill this out."

He pointed to a table across the chamber.

"I don't have a pen, either," Holbrook said.

The rat slumped, utterly destroyed by Holbrook's endless requests. Then he rummaged through his desk and held up a pen.

Holbrook hurried over to the table and began to fill out the form.

Name. Address. That was simple.

Previous shows. They wanted to know where else Holbrook had shown his paintings—like a museum or art gallery. Holbrook swallowed. Would they let him in if he hadn't ever had a show? He wasn't sure, so he filled in "Irving's Place." They had left a lot of blanks for previous shows, so after some anxious thought, he added, "Behind the Big Rocks." After all, Jagger had spied on him there and had seen a painting.

Holbrook took the application up to the rat.

The rat stared at it. "Irving's Place?"

Holbrook was suddenly very aware of his dusty backpack and dirty feet.

"Do you know that Corvus Cawfield is going to be here?" sniffed the rat.

Corvus Cawfield was one of the most famous artists in the world. Even Holbrook had heard of him, way out in the desert.

"And Andy Wartsnall," added the rat with a curl of his lip.

Holbrook swallowed. "It said newcomers, too."

He could feel his throat beating. What if, after all this, they wouldn't let him in?

"Squeak, what seems to be the problem?" said a warm, soft voice.

Holbrook turned around. Behind him stood a mink. He had delicate paws and silky dark brown fur. A single streak of gold ran from his snout to his ear. It gave him an unusual, elegant look. His dark eyes seemed gently amused.

The rat straightened quickly.

"Count Rumolde," he said.

"Is there a problem?" asked the mink again.

"He's a nobody," said Squeak. "And he wants in."

The mink smiled. "Newcomers, too," he reminded Squeak, then turned to Holbrook.

"What do you have?"

"A painting," Holbrook answered.

"Ahh." The mink looked at him with bright interest.

Holbrook could tell he wanted to see the painting. But Holbrook didn't want to be laughed at. Not here. Not before he even got to the Exhibition.

"Oils? Acrylic?" inquired the mink. Then he seemed to catch himself. "I'm terribly sorry. Allow me to introduce myself. I am Count Rainier Rumolde. I happen to be an art collector. Naturally, my curiosity is aroused at the thought of finding a bright new talent."

New talent? Holbrook hadn't quite thought of himself that way. Was he talented?

He glanced at the mink. He looked rich and fancy. He probably read a lot of books. An art collector would know about art.

Count Rumolde smiled, an encouraging smile.

"I could maybe show you," said Holbrook, bending down and unlacing his pack. He pulled out *Starry Sky*, unwrapped it from its cloth, and spread it open.

He waited for the laughs.

Count Rumolde said quietly, "It's lovely."

Holbrook looked up. Lovely? No one had ever said that before! The mink looked at him with dark, intense eyes.

"I call it *Starry Sky*."

"Quite extraordinary," said the count.

Holbrook's heart leapt at the word "extraordinary." Wasn't that what they were looking for: artistes extraordinaire?

"I—I thought I might enter it in the Exhibition," Holbrook said, nervously, still waiting for the laughs.

"Oh, you must," said the mink. "After all, the point is to find the world's *greatest* artists."

Holbrook suddenly felt himself trembling. Did Count Rumolde know what he was saying?

The mink looked at the painting again and asked, "Where are you staying?"

"Nowhere—I mean, I don't know. I hadn't really thought about it."

Holbrook blushed. He had come to the city totally unprepared. He hadn't thought through anything!

"Perhaps you would do me the honor of staying

at my place?" asked the mink. "It's quite spacious and near the Exhibition Hall. I would be so pleased. Truly. It's not often that one runs across such talent."

With each word, Holbrook felt his head get lighter and lighter. It was like water in the desert. "You must enter the Exhibition." "A painting like yours." "Such talent!"

Before Holbrook could answer, the count said, "Squeak, please get Mr. Holbrook's things."

The rat hurried out from behind the desk.

Holbrook clung tightly to his painting.

"Just the pack, of course," said Count Rumolde. "That," he said, pointing at *Starry Sky*, "is much too precious to let out of our sight."

Holbrook rolled it up again. Then, with the mink's paw a friendly guide around his shoulder, he allowed himself to be led from the hall.

Count Rumolde led the way to a tall apartment building of mustard-hued stone. High above the entrance, bright flags snapped in the breeze. Beneath them, carved in stone, was the name "The Mordred Arms."

Holbrook gazed upward. "You live here?" he asked.

"Actually, I own it," said the count simply, as if it was nothing to own a tall city building.

A plump bullfrog in a bright red doorman's uniform tipped his hat to Rumolde and held open the heavy glass doors.

The count strode in, and Holbrook followed. The bullfrog nodded at him and smiled.

Squeak scrambled in behind them with a frown.

The lobby was full of richly dressed creatures. Many glanced up to greet the count and stare with friendly interest at Holbrook.

"Here for the Exhibition," the mink explained as

they moved toward the elevators. "An extraordinary new artist."

There was that word again. "Extraordinary." He wasn't just an artist. He was an extraordinary artist!

They reached the elevator. It was a small private elevator—a cage of gilded metalwork shaped into leaves and curlicues. Holbrook had never been in an elevator.

Squeak pushed a button marked PENTHOUSE, and up they rose.

When the elevator stopped and the doors slid open, they stepped straight into an entryway gleaming with rich brown marble and heavy mirrors. Holbrook stared around him.

Another rat, this one slender and pleasant, greeted them with a slight nod and an enquiring look.

"Some refreshment, if you please, Grayler. Is there anything in particular you would like, Holbrook?"

"Huh?" Holbrook wasn't really listening because he was staring at a portrait of a stout lady mink with eyes that seemed to glare at him.

"My mother," explained Count Rumolde. "Looks just like her, I'm afraid. But the painting is rather pedestrian, don't you think? Not really in the same league as yours."

Holbrook nodded. He wasn't sure what "pedestrian" meant, but from Count Rumolde's tone he assumed it meant something quite different from extraordinary.

Count Rumolde turned to Squeak. "Please take

Mr. Holbrook's bag to his room. Perhaps *Starry Sky* as well?" With a reassuring smile, the mink held out his paw for the painting that Holbrook still clutched close. "It will be safest in your room, free from excess handling."

Holbrook hesitated.

Squeak rolled his eyes. "Who'd want it, anyway?" he muttered.

"Squeak!" scolded the count.

"Well, it's not like it's a real painting. Not like that," protested the scrawny rat, waving at the painting of Count Rumolde's mother, which indeed looked so real that it seemed you could almost reach out and touch one of her bristling whiskers. "His doesn't look like stars or sky or anything. It's just a bunch of squiggles. A baby could do it!"

Squiggles! Holbrook couldn't believe it. He'd come all the way to the city and nothing had changed!

"There you are wrong," said Count Rumolde sternly. "It is clear that Holbrook is an artist of great talent. His painting looks exactly as he intended it to look. I'm sure he could, if he wanted, paint anything to look like the real thing."

"Yeah, right," snorted Squeak.

"I can!" cried Holbrook. "It's easy."

Squeak pretended to cough to cover up his scornful laugh.

"If I had some paint, I'd show you!" Holbrook said.

"Actually," said Count Rumolde, "it just so happens that I do have paints and canvas. I dabble a bit in painting myself. Come see."

He led the way down several door-lined hallways to a studio in the south corner of the penthouse, where the light streamed in through high windows. The studio was equipped with fine brushes and racks of paints and a number of standing easels made of expensive-looking wood.

"As you can see, I'm but an amateur." The count waved dismissively at his paintings. There were stacks and stacks of them. His latest effort was of a bowl of fruit. He had tried to paint it at least a dozen times. Holbrook saw that one of the paintings had been tossed into a corner. The canvas was punched in and the frame in splinters.

"Would you?" Count Rumolde propped a blank canvas on an easel. "I would be truly honored to see a master at work."

Holbrook hesitated. He'd never painted in front of others. He always hid when he painted in the desert.

"Just as I thought," Squeak muttered.

Holbrook picked up a brush, thought for a moment and began to paint a scene he'd seen a thousand times back in Rattler's Bend.

It was the work of but an hour to capture a distant range of barren mountains, the lavish pinks and oranges of the setting sun, and a crooked Joshua tree silhouetted against the sky, seemingly almost as old as the setting sun itself.

"It looks just like it!" said Squeak, amazed.

"Indeed," said Count Rumolde, seemingly a bit amazed himself. "It's quite marvelous. Would you . . . could I induce you to allow me to display it for tonight's party?"

"Party?" asked Holbrook.

"Yes, just a small gathering of friends. Please say you'll join us and that you will allow me to show your *Desert Sunset. Starry Sky* must wait to be unveiled at the Exhibition, of course," added the count.

Desert Sunset wasn't anything special to Holbrook. He could do ones like it by the dozen; it didn't have any feelings in it. But both Count Rumolde and Squeak looked at him with such admiration that he couldn't help but be flattered. "Well, okay," he said. "You may put it on your wall if you like."

"Excellent!" exclaimed the mink.

Holbrook felt very grand giving his permission. So grand that he even let Squeak carry *Starry Sky* to his room for him.

*H*olbrook stood in the corner of the huge living room clutching a glass of sparkling cream soda. He'd never drunk cream soda, and it had a nice rich tingle to it. He sipped at it, being careful not to spill. The room was full of glamorous animals who mostly ignored him.

A lady bulldog dripping with fat pearls approached Holbrook. "I am the Duchess of Woof," she announced. "Are you somebody?"

Holbrook had to shake his head no.

She moved on.

Holbrook's *Desert Sunset* had replaced the portrait of Count Rumolde's mother on the wall near the elevator. He had been rather surprised to see that it was the only piece of art in the room, since the count had told him he collected art. But even so, no one noticed it.

"There's Corvus Cawfield," he heard someone say.

Holbrook craned his neck. He saw a large black crow talking with a serious-looking mole. The crow had a lively sparkle to his eyes. How Holbrook wished he had the courage to go up and talk to him.

A troupe of snails arrived. They proved to be a rowdy bunch, drinking a great deal of champagne and breaking into song at the least excuse.

Grayler, the butler, moved smoothly through the crowd offering small sandwiches and delicate bits of cheese.

Then Holbrook forgot about everything because at that moment the elevator doors opened and out stepped the prettiest creature he had ever seen. She was a slender frog with long, graceful legs. Her eyes, large and dark, were tender, yet there was something fierce and proud in them, too.

Other creatures turned to stare. A swan near Holbrook reared back her neck and hissed softly, "Margot Frogtayne!"

"The famous ballerina?" asked someone.

"The best in the world," barked the duchess.

"Well, that depends," replied a snippy-looking Chihuahua. "Perhaps the ballerina Ms. Swanson here would not agree."

The swan glared at the duchess. Clearly, she did not.

"The Exhibition will determine the best," said the Chihuahua.

But the duchess wasn't listening. Like others in the crowd, she seemed to have eyes only for the frog

and her companion, a large smiling snail with a silky bow tie around his neck.

Margot Frogtayne moved with grace into the foyer. She paused to look at Holbrook's painting.

Holbrook's throat pounded. How he wished it was *Starry Sky* that was hanging there! Something special and wonderful—something as special as she was.

The frog smiled and turned to the snail. *"C'est tres jolie, n'est pas, Enrico?"*

The snail nodded. He had a warm, pleasant face. When he spoke, his voice was deep and flowery. *"Molto bello,"* he said.

"What'd he say?" Holbrook eagerly asked the duchess. "What'd she say?"

"They said the painting is pretty, more or less," she growled.

They thought his painting was pretty! And now other animals were noticing it, too.

Count Rumolde rushed up to them, his paws held out. "Mademoiselle Margot, Signor Escargot! Welcome! I am honored. I see you are admiring my newest acquisition. Let me introduce you to the artist."

He waved a paw for Holbrook to join them.

All the animals now turned to stare at Holbrook.

Holbrook stood for a moment. The frog smiled at him. He stumbled forward.

"He's nobody," he heard the duchess say in answer to a question. She sounded rather angry.

"Holbrook, this is Mademoiselle Margot Frog-tayne. The world's greatest prima ballerina."

"Enchantée," the frog said modestly, turning her lovely eyes downward. She curved one pretty leg just a bit.

"I refuse to stay here and be insulted!" the swan trumpeted and flapped into the elevator.

Count Rumolde paid no attention.

"And this, of course, is Enrico Escargot."

Holbrook smiled anxiously at the snail; everyone else seemed to know who he was.

Enrico laughed. "You have not heard of the great Enrico Escargot?" He threw back his head, and in a voice surprisingly powerful for such a small creature (large as he was for a snail) he sang, *"Figaro! Figaro, Figaro, Figaro-oooh."*

When Holbrook still looked confused, the duchess barked, "Everyone knows Enrico, the world's greatest operatic tenor!"

Enrico Escargot smiled at Holbrook, "It is of no consequence, my friend. The world knows many things that are not important."

A large lobster crowded closer. He glared at Holbrook over tiny steel spectacles. "He doesn't know of Mademoiselle Frogtayne or Signor Escargot. Really, where have you been? Living under a rock?"

Holbrook blushed. Actually, his burrow *was* under a rock.

Enrico frowned and started to say something, but a number of animals, along with the lobster, crowded forward and pushed Holbrook aside. The Duchess of Woof nearly seized him with her jaws, so eager was she to get past him. Holbrook was forced back into his corner. He took a big gulp of his cream soda, but it was warm and had lost its bubbles.

T h e party grew more and more crowded, and the throng grew louder and louder. Enrico Escargot and the other snails, who turned out to be his opera company from across the Northern Sea, roared out one song after another.

A woodpecker and a mallard started squawking at each other about who was the best sculptor in the world. They began to viciously peck each other, until Grayler, the butler, pulled them apart. Holbrook couldn't believe that these were some of the finest artists in the world. They were as bad as Crink and Crank back home arm wrestling at Irving's to see who was the strongest!

Holbrook inched through the crowd, hoping to spot Margot, but it was impossible to see over all the other animals. Then, suddenly, there she was. Right next to him, standing as gracefully as a lily.

"Monsieur Holbrook. There you are," she said. "I wanted to apologize for Homarus Cray Lobster. He is an art critic and is too important in his own mind."

"Oh, it's all right," Holbrook said. The lobster was right. He *had* been living under a rock. He didn't know anything. Margot would soon find out how unimportant he really was.

"You are a friend of Count Rumolde's?" she asked, looking at him rather curiously.

"Oh, yes," he declared, hoping she would think more of him.

She nodded. "He knows many famous creatures."

Holbrook felt himself swell a bit. "I'm here for the Exhibition," he said, trying to make it sound as if he was an important artist, like all the other creatures in the room. And maybe he would be!

"Yes, your painting is lovely."

Holbrook wanted to say that it wasn't the one for the Exhibition, but suddenly he wondered what Margot Frogtayne or any of these other famous creatures would think of *Starry Sky*. Count Rumolde liked it, but would the others think it was just squiggles? Everyone seemed to like *Desert Sunset* so much.

He swallowed and nodded. "Thank you," he said.

Just then the lobster scuttled up again. "Mademoiselle, I implore you to join our group." He waved a feeler toward several animals by the window, including Corvus Cawfield. "The important animals are over there. The riffraff will swallow up all your time, if you let them." He clicked a large dismissive claw at Holbrook.

Margot stared angrily at the lobster, then turned to

Holbrook and said, "I must talk with Corvus about plans for the Exhibition, but I would be honored to show you the sights of Golden City tomorrow, if I might."

The lobster blinked in surprise. "Surely, you're not serious, Mademoiselle. No one knows him. He could be a tramp, a thief. Or worse!"

"Mais non," said Margot. "He is none of those things. I can tell. Besides Enrico will be with me." She turned back to Holbrook and said softly, "Tomorrow, then?"

Holbrook swallowed and nodded, unable to speak, but as Margot turned away, the lobster steering her through the crowd, he suddenly shouted, "Tomorrow!"

Someone laughed. But it was a nice laugh.

All the animals around him seemed to be smiling. He suddenly remembered that he was in Golden City, in a fancy apartment on top of a big building with the finest creatures in the world! Just as in one of his books!

How their jewels glittered and gleamed. How their eyes glistened and their words sparkled. How beautiful Margot the frog was.

He found himself singing with Enrico's troupe and eating little sandwiches and carrots cut up to look like flowers. He even kissed the duchess's heavy paw!

The city. The city. All dreams did come true in the city.

Then, suddenly, Holbrook realized he was terribly

tired. What a long, long day it had been since he had left Rattler's Bend.

He slipped from the living room and stumbled sleepily down a hushed hallway to his room.

He thought he saw the flash of a rat's tail at the end of his corridor. Squeak?

As soon as he closed the door to his room, Holbrook checked under his bed, where he had hidden *Starry Sky*. It was fine.

He climbed into bed and gratefully slipped between the silken sheets. What if the animals of Rattler's Bend could see him now? And they thought he was just finger painting!

"Lovely." That's what Margot had said. Of course, she'd only seen *Desert Sunset*. But even so, Holbrook smiled. Then yawned.

His thoughts tumbled toward darkness, but the last thing he remembered were Margot's eyes, sparkling and tender, and her voice saying softly, "Tomorrow."

10

"You were a triumph!" declared Count Rumolde. "Everyone was talking about the young lizard and his wonderful painting of the desert sunset."

It was the next morning, and the silky mink strolled proudly about his living room reliving the night before.

"They were?" asked Holbrook.

"Oh, yes," said the count. "Just think, one day in the city, and already you are the talk of the town."

It *was* amazing. Here he was sitting high above the city on a soft velvet sofa, full of fine food, with a famous art collector praising him. The talk of the town! He had no idea it would be so easy to become a famous artist.

"Mademoiselle Frogtayne, in particular, admired it," said Count Rumolde.

Holbrook could feel a silly grin on his face.

The mink smiled warmly, as if sharing in Holbrook's love. "She said she wished she had one just like it."

"She did?" said Holbrook.

"Of course I told her that was impossible. A great artist like yourself would not paint the same picture a second time."

He brushed a paw over his streak of golden fur and glanced at Holbrook.

"I could give it to her," said Holbrook, eagerly nodding at his painting on the wall.

"Give her *my* painting?" said Rumolde.

"Your painting?"

"Of course," said Rumolde.

Suddenly, Holbrook was confused. He hadn't thought he was giving the painting to the mink. But then he remembered that he had used Count Rumolde's paints and canvas and had painted it in his studio.

"Margot Frogtayne really said she wanted one?" Holbrook asked again.

The count nodded as if not much interested. He turned away and began to feed something the color of blood to an exotic orchid plant near the window. A single purple streak striped its white petals, just like Count Rumolde's one streak of golden fur.

"I suppose I could do another."

"Hmm?" The mink glanced up. "I'm sorry, I didn't hear you."

Holbrook's throat felt a little dry, so he swallowed and said a little louder, "I could do another *Desert Sunset.*"

"Margot will be delighted!" declared Count

Rumolde. And with his soft paws, he steered Holbrook down the hall to the studio.

Holbrook painted another *Desert Sunset.* He tried to put something special into it because it was for Margot, but Count Rumolde insisted he do it exactly like the one the day before, reminding him again and again how much Margot wanted one just like it.

At last Holbrook was finished. The painting had gone quickly enough, but it had felt a little like doing the dishes at Irving's.

Then, to his surprise, Count Rumolde set another blank canvas on the easel.

"The Duchess of Woof wanted one as well—you remember her, the bulldog. Your painting had many admirers last night."

"*Another* one?" cried Holbrook.

"The duchess is one of the judges for the Exhibition," said Count Rumolde. "She will remember your generosity."

"No," said Holbrook, setting down his brush.

"This is how you win exhibitions," Count Rumolde said. "You make friends. You do favors."

Holbrook shook his head. It didn't feel right.

"A famous ballerina like Margot Frogtayne is not interested in being friends with a nobody," Count Rumolde said quietly.

Holbrook hesitated.

"It will take nothing. A mere bit of your time. It's easy for you," the mink added as he glanced at his own half-finished painting of the bowl of fruit.

And Holbrook saw something flash in the count's eyes that made him uneasy. But he was right. It *was* easy and, perhaps, that's the way it worked in the city. Small favors to the right creatures.

He quickly did another *Desert Sunset*.

Count Rumolde gave his neck a friendly squeeze. "You are a fast learner," he said. "This is the way to become somebody. You'll see."

11

When Holbrook got back to his room, he realized that even though Count Rumolde was sleek and well spoken, even though he lived in a fabulous penthouse and had parties for famous creatures, he wished he could stay somewhere else. Holbrook didn't like the hungry gleam in the mink's eyes when he looked at Holbrook's paintings. He didn't like how the count thought nothing of painting the same thing over and over.

But where could he go? He didn't know anyone. He didn't think a hotel would let him stay for nothing. He glanced to the street below his window. Hard sidewalks and dark alleys. He couldn't stay on the streets.

He paced his room restlessly. Outside, the sky was blue. The city was pink and beige and beckoning. He longed to see more of it. Margot Frogtayne had said she would show him the city today, but would she remember? He had no idea how to get hold of her.

Perhaps he could go out for just a breath of air. But what should he do with *Starry Sky*? If he took it with him, it might get damaged. But he didn't like the idea of leaving it here. He didn't know why he was worried. What use was it to Count Rumolde? At last, he settled on moving the painting to the back of his closet and carefully locking the door behind him with a key the count had given him.

He almost felt as if he was escaping when he pushed through the heavy glass doors of the Mordred Arms and out onto the bright, bustling streets of Golden City.

He heard a joyful *clang! clang!* and realized that one of the famous Golden City cable cars had stopped right in front of the building.

It was crowded with animals who sat on the benches or clung to straps that hung from the roof.

"Monsieur Holbrook! *Alors!*"

He saw Margot Frogtayne and Enrico Escargot on the cable car. They were shouting and waving to him!

"We were just coming for you! Come join us!"

Holbrook darted into the street, leapt aboard, and grabbed a handrail just as the car swooped off.

"Bravo!" cried Enrico Escargot.

Holbrook sat down next to Margot Frogtayne.

"Bonjour," she said with a smile.

Holbrook was pretty sure that meant hello. And he smiled back, his throat pulsing with joy.

The cable car turned a sharp corner and began to

climb a steep hill. Far below sparkled the bay. The cable car was at such a slant that Margot slid right into him. She laughed, and Holbrook blushed.

Up and up and up they went, and then over the hill and down with clangs and the squeal of the hand brake and the shouts of excited tourists.

At the end of the line, they hopped off. The Golden City Wharf was crowded with restaurants, bustling tourists, and souvenir stands. The air was damp with sea spray and the smell of seaweed. Everywhere vendors beckoned, hoping to sell postcards and coffee mugs and T-shirts that said, "World's Greatest Ant" and "My Grandpuppy Can Lick Anyone."

Margot linked her arm in Holbrook's, and the threesome happily strolled along the waterfront, chatting.

Holbrook didn't think there was much to say about the Great Desert, but Enrico and Margot seemed fascinated and urged him to talk. Margot was amazed at Holbrook's descriptions of the sandstorms and the cactus.

"You are perhaps a cowboy?" asked Enrico. "You ride wild coyotes and shoot six guns?"

Margot looked at him with glowing eyes, and Holbrook, who did none of those things, found himself nodding and saying things like "I reckon" and calling Margot "little lady" and Enrico "pardner."

"And to be an artist, too!" said Enrico. "This is a great thing, my friend. To show the world *your* world. Is not that true art?"

Holbrook didn't mention that no one he knew wanted to see his squiggly world. Instead, he hinted that he was quite famous in certain desert circles.

"Officially, I'm known as Holbrook the Lesser," he said.

"Since I'm a lesser earless lizard." He added, "That's my artist name."

They sat on the edge of the breakwater and looked at the sea. It was as big as the desert. Maybe bigger. And blue and gray and white and maybe a million other colors. He sighed happily. "I've never seen the ocean before," Holbrook said. "I guess there are a lot of things I haven't seen."

"It is a big world," agreed Enrico.

That's what Irving had said, too. For a moment, Holbrook felt a flash of homesickness, but then the snail continued, "You must tell us about your paintings."

Forever after, Holbrook would remember that afternoon. While the seagulls wheeled and the waves lip-lapped against the wall, he talked as he had never talked before. The words spilled out of him as if they had been waiting a long time.

He talked about the big thing inside of him, about how it wouldn't stay inside. He told them about *Starry Sky,* told them that it was a real painting. And he hoped a real artist would look at it and see that, too. Enrico and Margot nodded and smiled and sighed. They understood!

"I know this big thing," said the snail. "When I

open my mouth and sing, it is this thing. It cannot be contained, no?"

Margot nodded, then jumped up and turned in a graceful pirouette. Slowly and perfectly. She knew about the thing inside, too.

As they strolled back toward the cable car, Holbrook thought this would be a good time to tell her how he had made a copy of *Desert Sunset* for her.

He was about to open his mouth when he noticed a long row of tourist paintings propped against the seawall. They were sad things. Whoever painted them didn't care about them. There was nothing in the paintings that spoke of feelings or hopes or dreams or big things. Just painting after painting of crashing ocean waves and still mountain lakes and fluffy kittens all looking the same.

Then Holbrook slowed and stopped. He was staring at his own painting! *Desert Sunset.* In fact, he was staring at *three* of them! The three he had painted for Count Rumolde were propped there in the middle of all the other paintings, with little sales tags on them!

"Oh, look. Eez not that your painting, Holbrook?" asked Margot. "But there is another one, too? And another." She sounded puzzled.

"I—I made it for *you,*" Holbrook stammered.

And for the duchess, he thought, but he didn't mention that. What were they doing here?

Suddenly, he had a horrible feeling about *Starry Sky.*

"I have to go," he said.

He began to hurry through the crowd, desperate to get back to the Mordred Arms.

"But Monsieur Holbrook, what eez it?" cried Margot.

"Wait, we will come, too!" shouted Enrico.

"I'm sorry," Holbrook shouted and ran on.

He had to get to the Mordred Arms. He hoped he wasn't too late.

12

Starry Sky was gone!

Holbrook stared at the empty space in the closet. He checked under the bed. He went back to look again in the closet. The painting wasn't anywhere in his room.

Just then Grayler swung open the bedroom door.

"Count Rumolde will see you now," he said, as if Holbrook had an appointment.

"He'd better," sputtered Holbrook.

Grayler led the way to the count's studio.

"Ah, there you are," said Count Rumolde casually as Grayler ushered Holbrook in. He wore an artist smock and stood before a canvas. It looked as if he had been working hard; paint stained his sharp claws.

"Where's my painting?" Holbrook cried. "What have you done with it?"

"Well, *Desert Sunset*—or should I say your *Desert Sunset*s are in the hands of three happy tourists. I've just been informed that they sold quickly and for

56

more than the usual price. I think we have a hit on our hands."

"A hit? What are you talking about?" Holbrook scanned the studio. There was no sign of *Starry Sky*.

"The tourists like your *Desert Sunset*. And I like whatever they like. I expect a hundred more, and then we'll see."

Holbrook felt terribly confused.

"I just want *Starry Sky* back."

"Yes, yes. You will get *Starry Sky* back. But first I need payment."

Count Rumolde dabbled a bit of red onto an apple. He was trying to paint the bowl of fruit again.

"It doesn't gleam," he muttered. "It never gleams. Does it need white, yellow, pink? What does it need?"

He looked over at Holbrook as if seeking his answer.

"Payment?" Holbrook still didn't understand.

"Of course. For your food and a place to stay."

"But you invited me," said Holbrook. "I'm a guest!"

"Is that so, Grayler?" asked the count.

"Not that I know of," replied the well-groomed rat.

"By my calculations, you owe me a hundred more *Desert Sunset*s."

A hundred paintings of the exact same thing? "I could never do that!" Holbrook cried.

"Then I shall take *Starry Sky* as payment instead." The count turned back to his painting. "Not that it's worth much. It doesn't even look like a real sky."

Grayler snickered, just the way Squeak had. Holbrook couldn't believe it! Count Rumolde had said it was special. He'd said it was "extraordinary."

"Squiggles," the mink said with a shake of his head, and then he suddenly snickered, joining with Grayler.

"I'll go to the police!" cried Holbrook. His heart was breaking. It wasn't any different in the city after all! But he'd never show Count Rumolde that he cared what he thought.

"What? And tell them that you've eaten my food and stayed in a room I provided for you and that now you refuse to pay?" He picked up his brush again. "Blue? Is it blue? Will blue make the apple come alive?"

Holbrook realized he was trapped. It was his word against those of Count Rumolde and Grayler—sophisticated creatures far more experienced than he in the ways of the city.

"All right," Holbrook said, his tail slumping. "I'll paint whatever you want."

He started for an easel.

"Not here," said the count sharply. "Not in the studio. This is where *I* paint."

He suddenly swept his canvas of fruit to the floor and grabbed Holbrook's arm and bared his short, sharp teeth. "What does it need!" he snarled. "You know, but you won't tell. You have it inside you, but you won't share it!"

"I—I don't know what you're talking about," Holbrook stammered.

Then the mink blinked, and he was Count Rumolde again. Calm and cool.

"Take him to the factory," he said to Grayler.

13

Grayler led Holbrook to the small service elevator, which was around the corner from the gilded guest elevator Holbrook had ridden in before. Inside the dark, smelly elevator, the rat punched a button marked B.

Holbrook watched as the floor numbers lit up above the doors. 22 ... 15 ... 10 ... L for lobby, B for basement.

The doors slid open to reveal a cement hall. A short way down the hall was a heavy metal door. When Grayler pushed it open, it scraped against the floor with a mournful screech.

They stepped inside a big gray room that smelled of mold and paint. It was filled with dozens of easels. At each easel, an animal artist was hurriedly painting. A few of them glanced up when Grayler and Holbrook stepped in, but most kept their eyes on their canvases, painting even faster as Grayler approached.

They stopped by a pale brown river otter, who was painting a mountain lake. The otter put the finishing touches to a pine tree, and set the painting next to several others that looked just like it.

The otter slid his eyes over to look at Holbrook, then quickly slid them away.

A tiny field mouse scurried back and forth across the lip of her easel, laying down a painting of a flowery meadow.

"That's supposed to be yellow," said Grayler, pointing out where she had put a red flower. "Change it! Now!"

The mouse bobbed her head and changed the color.

A pug dog with a black muzzle and patient eyes carefully painted the whiskers on an orange and white kitten. At his feet were half a dozen paintings of the exact same kitten playing with the exact same ball of blue yarn.

Grayler waved at an easel holding a blank canvas. "Here's your station," he said to Holbrook.

On a little stand next to the easel were several brushes and a palette with paint already laid on it: all the colors he would need for *Desert Sunset,* and nothing more.

"Get to work."

The sleek rat strode away, the heavy metal door clanging shut behind him.

"Hello," Holbrook said to the pug.

"Silence!" A huge mountain dog suddenly rose up

from the floor and barked in a booming voice. "Keep working, all of you!"

The pug glanced over at Holbrook, gave him a gentle smile, and went back to his kittens.

Holbrook picked up a brush. He wanted to paint something black and boiling and angry. But he would never get *Starry Sky* back if he did. He swallowed hard and picked up his palette knife. He mixed red and blue and white. Purples and pinks and reds. Pretty sunsets. That's what he had to paint.

He worked steadily and silently, like the other animals. He was finishing up his third painting when the mountain dog barked, "Break time!"

All the animals set down their brushes. Suddenly, the room was abuzz with voices.

The pug turned to him with a friendly smile, "Maxwell's the name. I see you're desert sunsets."

Holbrook nodded and introduced himself.

"I'm kittens," said the pug. "It may seem odd for a dog, but to tell you the truth, I love kittens. They're so soft and fluffy and playful, don't you think?"

Maxwell led Holbrook toward a room off the factory floor.

Dozens of animals streamed in, past long gray tables and benches, to a counter, where they picked up a tray of food.

A cross-looking weasel slopped food onto the trays.

"That's Frick," whispered Maxwell. "Stay away from him if you can."

"We need more beans!" the weasel shouted over his shoulder.

A short, fat ape in a dirty white chef's hat thrust his face through the kitchen opening. He scowled at the weasel.

"You come and get the beans," he cried. "I am the chef. Not a serving boy. Not a lackey. Not a minion. I am the greatest chef in the world, and what do I get to work with? Beans!"

"Who's that?" asked Holbrook trying not to stare. Of all the unusual animals he'd met in the city, the ape was the rarest.

"He's an orangutan Rumolde found wandering the streets. He calls himself Maurice LeMonde," whispered Maxwell. "He thinks he's a famous chef. But his cooking is awful."

"He's mad," murmured the rabbit next to Holbrook. "Loony."

"Crazy as a March hare," agreed a chipmunk. The rabbit glared, but several other animals giggled.

Perhaps Maurice heard them, because he suddenly cried, "I am not a clown. I am not a circus act. I am not a buffoon placed here for your amusement. I am the chef!" And then he disappeared back into the kitchen.

"I don't suppose you've earned any food yet," Maxwell said.

"You mean, we have to pay for this?" Holbrook said, looking at his tray. Grayish beans, lumpy rice, soggy bread, and a blob of green Jell-O.

"We have to pay for everything," said Maxwell.

A snippy sparrow checked off each animal on a list as it went through the line.

"I'll pay for yours," Maxwell said. "What's a little more debt? I'm a hundred kittens in the hole already, anyway."

"Thanks," said Holbrook. "I'll pay you back."

The sparrow cocked a bright black eye at him, gave a short sharp laugh, and made two check marks next to Maxwell's name.

14

Holbrook joined Maxwell and some other animals at a long metal table. He could see a bit of the sidewalk through the high barred windows that ran along one basement wall. It was nearly dark outside, and he realized it had been a long time since he had eaten. He was starved! He spooned a big bite into his mouth . . . the beans and rice stuck to his throat, tasteless and lumpy. He could barely swallow them.

Suddenly, he wondered where he would spend the night, but as if in answer, Maxwell said, "There's an empty cot next to mine."

"You sleep here, too?" asked Holbrook.

"For a price," said Maxwell. "You have to earn it."

"And you never catch up," whispered the mouse sitting nearby. "You have to paint to pay them off, but each day that you paint costs you more in room and board."

Holbrook stared at the mouse. She looked old and

worn out. "How long have you been here?" He hardly dared ask.

"Over a thousand meadow paintings," she answered, her small paws trembling.

"Why don't you just leave?" he asked. "It isn't right. They can't make you stay, can they?"

Neither animal spoke, because just then the big mountain dog came strolling by. He stopped next to Holbrook.

"So you're the new one?" the dog said. "Desert sunsets, I hear. Never liked the desert myself. I like mountains. Do you like mountains? You'd better like mountains."

Holbrook nodded nervously.

"My name's Ironlung. . . . Know why they call me Ironlung?"

Holbrook shook his head. He could feel the warm breath of the dog on his face.

"I sound the alarm. Anyone tries to get out of their obligation—say, by sneaking away in the middle of the night—I let the world know about it, and we come and take you back."

Ironlung nodded toward several dogs and rats who stood by the doorways or walked about the room. "Are you going to run out on your obligation?" he asked.

"But I didn't know—" Holbrook started to say.

"You ate the food, didn't you," interrupted Ironlung, staring at Holbrook's barely touched plate. Then he reared up and roared out in a deafening voice. "Everybody listen up! What time is it, Maxwell? What time of year?"

Maxwell seemed to know the answer Ironlung wanted.

"Tourist season," said the pug, not looking at Ironlung. "*High* tourist season."

"And what does that mean?" barked Ironlung.

"We work late," Maxwell said in a soft, steady voice.

"That's right!" barked Ironlung. "The Exhibition is less than a week away. The town is full of art lovers. And that's what we're going to give them. Art—art by the yard, art by the caseload, art by the truckload. Everyone back to work."

All the animals groaned, then quickly fell silent as the guards glared.

Out they went, back to the workroom.

Holbrook lost track of the number of *Desert Sunsets* he did. At first he tried to make each one just a little bit different. It was kind of a game to see if he could sneak it by the guards. But after a while he stopped trying to do even that. It was easier just to slap them out. After all, he had to do 100 just to get *Starry Sky* back, and with every second he stayed in the Mordred Arms, with every morsel he ate, he owed them more paintings!

At last, Ironlung called a halt to the work. A late, lonely feeling chilled the air. Everyone laid down brushes and trudged wearily off to the various sleeping rooms, too tired to talk.

Holbrook collapsed onto a thin cot next to Maxwell's. His eyes burned. His fingers ached. He never wanted to paint another desert sunset as long as he lived.

"I wonder how many I owe now," he said.

"More than you started with," said the pug. "That's the way they work it."

"We could escape," said Holbrook.

"It's been tried," said Maxwell. "I tried it myself."

"What happened?" asked Holbrook.

There was a long pause before the pug answered. "It's not a good idea."

"I wish I'd never come to Golden City!" Holbrook suddenly burst out.

"Know what I wish?" said Maxwell, his gentle eyes staring at the ceiling. "I wish just once I could paint a gray kitten."

Late that night, Holbrook woke up. Or maybe it was a dream that found him awake on his cot staring out the doorway into the dimly lit hallway. Something rustled out there, and he saw—or maybe he dreamed—that Frick, the weasel, crept past carrying something in his hand.

It caught the light, and Holbrook saw that it was a great sharp knife.

Maxwell murmured in his sleep. Holbrook glanced over at him, then back to the hall. Maybe he *had* dreamed it, after all. There was no Frick; there was no knife. Only dim shadows in an empty hallway.

15

The next day, after a breakfast of beans ("Beans for breakfast!" exclaimed Holbrook) and sour-tasting milk, the animals were herded back into the work-room and immediately put to work.

Lunch was more beans. A mole who, oddly enough, painted ocean waves, squinted at his plate and protested, "Beans, *again?*"

Maurice poked his head out and cried, "Beans. Yes, beans. That's all they give me! I am the chef. Not a magician. Not a conjurer. Not a miracle worker. I cannot turn beans into ratatouille!"

"You can't even turn beans into beans," muttered the mole.

The ape bared his teeth angrily, then seemed to remember something, because he suddenly said, "Just wait. You will see my greatness. Rumolde has prom-ised." Then with a wicked gleam in his eye, he drew back into the kitchen.

Holbrook tried to swallow a few more bites of

food but gave up. All too soon he and the others were filing back to the workroom and more paintings.

They were so busy that it was late afternoon before Holbrook had a moment to lift his head. He stared up at the barred windows. He could see the feet of animals as they passed by on their way home for the evening. A young mouse bent down and peered into the room.

He tugged on his mother's sleeve, but she didn't notice or didn't care. Holbrook saw the little mouse stumble as his mother pulled him away.

Once again, Holbrook wondered if there was any way out of the factory.

In between paintings, he carefully studied the room. There were three doors. The metal one Grayler had brought him through yesterday; a second door that Holbrook now knew led to the cafeteria and their sleeping quarters; and a door that led to a back room. A thin-tailed squirrel continually darted in and out of that room, reloading the animals' palettes with the colors they needed when they ran out of paint.

Holbrook wondered if the back room led anywhere.

As the squirrel worked, he kept glancing nervously at Ironlung. Often, he got the colors wrong—giving the mouse red when there was no red in her meadow and Holbrook the wrong blue. Ironlung shouted angrily at him because it slowed things down.

The third time the squirrel got it wrong, Holbrook cautiously approached the big dog.

"Back to your station!" Ironlung barked.

Holbrook's throat pulsed. "I could do it," he quickly said.

"Do what? What could you do?" growled Ironlung.

"I could put the paint on the palettes," he said. "I've been watching. I know what each painter needs."

"We need you on *Desert Sunsets*," said Ironlung.

"I'm ahead," said Holbrook. He was. He had so many paintings drying that there wasn't any more room to stack them next to his easel.

Just then the mole complained, "I don't use black. I need green."

The squirrel had it wrong again.

"You've slowed us down for the last time!" roared Ironlung to the trembling squirrel. "You're out of here."

"Please," whispered the squirrel. "Please don't send me . . . *there*."

The word "there" fell like a cold stone in the room. From it came silence and fear. Holbrook wondered what "there" was. He saw Maxwell stiffen and shudder at the word.

"I could paint more fall leaves," the squirrel said quickly. "Put me back to painting. I'll work late. I'll work all night!"

"I ask you, are fall leaves selling?" Ironlung's voice was low and dangerous. "Are they?"

"I—I don't know," stammered the squirrel.

"The answer is no," roared the dog. "Nobody wants fall leaves."

"You," he pointed at Holbrook. "You do the palettes."

"No!" shrieked the squirrel. "Please." He fell to his thin knees, his teeth chattering with fear.

Holbrook was horrified.

"He could do spring leaves," cried Holbrook. "Everyone likes spring."

"Yes!" squeaked the squirrel. "I can do spring leaves. I'm sure I can."

Two dogs were already converging on the squirrel, but Ironlung raised his paw.

"I'll give you one more chance," he snapped at the squirrel. "And you," he growled at Holbrook. "Get going!"

16

Holbrook quickly ran about grabbing any palette that was low on paint. He dashed into the back room. It was full of supplies. Hundreds of blank canvases stood stacked on the floor. Tubes of paint in dozens and dozens of different colors filled the shelves.

Normally, Holbrook would have been enchanted. He'd never seen so many colors. The air was heavy with his favorite smell, the dusky scent of paint and oil. Normally, the empty canvases would have beckoned like worlds he could step into. But not now.

He remembered what each animal needed and quickly squeezed out big blobs of paint on each of the palettes. As he did, he studied the supply room. No windows, no door, no vents. He raced back to the workroom. All the animals were painting as fast as they could. The squirrel shot him a grateful glance as Holbrook set down a palette of yellows and greens and white.

Holbrook raced back to the supply room. Again,

he scanned the walls, the floor, the ceiling. Nothing.

He filled the palettes and scurried back to the workroom. Was there only one way out? The door to the hallway, watched by half a dozen guards?

He looked at Ironlung. The big dog yawned a head-splitting yawn, smacked his lips, and blinked. He was clearly sleepy. The weasels and other guard dogs looked bored and half-asleep themselves. They didn't really expect the prisoners to try anything.

Maybe it could be done.

Holbrook hurried around the workroom picking up more empty palettes. Maxwell looked startled when Holbrook picked up his. It still had plenty of yellow and orange, but the pug didn't say anything.

When Holbrook came back from the supply room, he set Maxwell's palette next to him and whispered, "Can you make a commotion?"

Maxwell stared at him.

"You'll never make it. They'll send you . . . *there*."

"I have to try," said Holbrook.

Maxwell glanced at Ironlung. His wrinkled brow looked even more wrinkled, but he nodded firmly. "You can count on me." He looked down at his palette, then back up at Holbrook with sudden tears in his eyes. There on his palette was a giant blob of kitten-gray paint.

Holbrook made his way through the aisles of easels until he was closest to the metal door to the hall. He saw Maxwell glance his way.

"Hey, that's my paintbrush!" the robin who painted daffodils next to Maxwell suddenly chirped. "He's got my paintbrush."

"What's going on?" said Ironlung, getting up abruptly.

"Give it back!" squawked the robin.

"What are you talking about," protested Maxwell, flinging his arms and stepping back into the easel behind him.

The mouse on the easel's lip flew into the air. She landed on the otter's mountain lake, and slid down the painting, clawing all the way.

"Watch it!" cried the otter, lunging for the mouse. His easel crashed into the rabbit, who jumped back and punched his foot through an ocean-wave painting on the floor.

The mole squealed furiously, and the room exploded in an uproar.

The guards raced for Maxwell and the squawking robin and the otter and the rabbit, who had suddenly started kicking at everyone. Holbrook quietly stepped to the door. It was heavy. Heavier than he expected, but he grabbed the handle, throwing himself backward as hard as he could.

Every head shot around at the sound of its loud scrape, but Holbrook was already through the narrow opening and darting down the hallway with all his speed.

"Aaaaarooooooo!" Ironlung let out an enraged cry.

Holbrook raced to the end of the corridor, turned

left, then right, and left again. The basement was a maze. He had no idea where he should go.

"*Aaaaarooooo!*" Ironlung was after him.

Holbrook saw a heavy fire door. It had to lead outside. He yanked on the door handle, but it wouldn't move. The door was locked! He ran as fast as he could on down the hall, but the howls grew closer.

He saw another door with an exit sign. He ran toward it. Ironlung and several sharp-faced dogs turned the corner and charged at him. Ironlung was in the lead, spit flying from his mouth.

Holbrook grabbed the doorknob and turned. The door opened onto a flight of stairs. He scrambled up them, Ironlung right behind. The dog's claws clattered on the hard steps. At the top of the stairs was a swinging door.

Holbrook charged through it into the sudden, startled hush of the sparkling lobby. Well-dressed animals turned and stared.

Holbrook stood panting and shaking.

Ironlung burst through the door behind him and skidded to a halt.

"What's going on," demanded the manager, a dignified cockatoo, bristling his head feathers. "I'm afraid you're disturbing the other tenants."

"I was just leaving," said Holbrook hurrying for the big glass doors.

Ironlung stood near the basement door, paralyzed by the watching eyes of the other animals. But coming across the lobby toward Holbrook with out-

stretched paws and a wide fake smile on his blunt muzzle was Rumolde.

The frog doorman pulled open the doors for Holbrook with a bow. Holbrook rushed toward them.

"My dear Holbrook, surely you're not leaving!" exclaimed Rumolde, rushing toward the doors, too.

They reached the doors together.

Rumolde hooked a clawed paw onto Holbrook's arm. Holbrook glanced at the watching tenants in the lobby. Rumolde followed his glance and reluctantly removed his paw. "You'll never see *Starry Sky* again," he whispered. "I'll tear it to threads."

Starry Sky!

Holbrook hesitated. Rumolde's nose was close to his ear. He could feel the mink's warm breath, quick now with the anticipation of leading Holbrook back to his art prison.

Holbrook shuddered, then turned and dashed out onto the darkening city street.

17

Holbrook raced along, turning down this street and that, paying no attention to where he went. Finally, he slowed and stopped. He couldn't run anymore. He looked around him. There was no sign of Rumolde or his servants.

He was in a part of town he hadn't seen before. It was raining, a soft, misty sort of rain that seemed to seep from the gray air itself. Broken glass and scraps of paper littered the sidewalk. It was nearly dark now, and a few streetlights flickered fitfully to life.

A thin black cat slipped past, pressed close to the wall. Holbrook drew back with alarm, but the cat's eyes were milky, and her head trembled as if she hadn't the strength to hold it still.

He shivered. It was really raining now. Cold hard drops that fell like a gray curtain past the yellow streetlights. Where could he go? He noticed a dark entryway with an overhang and dodged into it. At least it was dry.

He sat in a corner and stared out at the night.

He was hungry and cold and alone. But at least he didn't have to paint any more *Desert Sunsets*. Then the thought came to him, What about Maxwell and all the others still trapped in the factory? What about the tired mouse and the frightened squirrel?

He needed to tell someone! He needed to set them free. But he realized it would have to wait for morning. He was in a strange, empty neighborhood. It was dark, late, and pouring rain. And, he suddenly realized, he was very tired.

He lay down on the hard cement, and curled his tail around him.

"Don't worry," he whispered, imagining that his words might somehow reach Maxwell. "I'll get you out."

18

The next morning, Holbrook uncurled himself, stretching out his stiff tail, and glanced about. Maybe there was a police station nearby. He could tell them about the factory. As he hurried down the street, looking for signs of life, he realized he smelled something wonderful. Fried onions, perhaps? With just a hint of garlic?

He felt dizzy. How long since he had eaten? Really eaten? He'd had only a few bites of Maurice's beans and rice for the last few days. He needed food.

He followed his nose to an alley. The smell was coming from there.

"Crumbs for the poor?" a voice cooed near his ear.

Holbrook jumped, then relaxed. It was just the three scrawny pigeons he'd met his first day in the city.

"It's the snake with legs," said One Leg.

"He has lived," said Lone Eye, sounding disappointed.

Scabs sighed and looked down at her feet.

"I'm hungry," announced Holbrook. There seemed no point in being modest with these three.

"What happened to your crusts?" said Lone Eye.

"I lost them," admitted Holbrook. "I lost everything," he mumbled.

He thought about telling them about Rumolde's art factory, but what could they do? They seemed even worse off than he was. At least, he wasn't begging . . . not yet.

Holbrook could still smell a delicious something in the air.

"Do you know where I could get some food?" he asked.

"Noooo, noooo," they murmured not meeting his eye, but Scabs glanced down the alley.

Holbrook walked that way. There, beside a Dumpster, was an open door. From it wafted the delicious smell. It was the back of a restaurant. A small bulldog thrust his head out the door and glared up and down the alley before tossing some garbage into the overflowing Dumpster.

Holbrook was so hungry he went right up to him. "Excuse me," he said, swallowing nervously. His stomach twisted painfully as he drew closer to the smells. "I don't really know how to begin . . ." How embarrassing this all was! Now he *was* begging! "But, you see, I have no money. And I haven't eaten in a while, I—"

"Can you wash dishes or not?" growled the bulldog.

Holbrook blinked, then nodded. He could wash dishes. He stepped into the warm, steamy kitchen. The bulldog looked him up and down, grunted, and said, "Name's Hammett."

"Holbrook," said Holbrook.

Hammett nodded toward a big metal sink heaped with dirty plates and silverware. "My regular dishwasher didn't show. The skunk."

Holbrook didn't know if Hammett was calling the old dishwasher names or if he really was a skunk.

Hammett snapped on a bright blue flame under a gas burner, grabbed a skillet from above his head, slammed it on the burner, and lobbed a thumb's worth of butter into the pan. The butter sizzled and bubbled, and Holbrook licked his dry lips.

"Hit that switch. The one on the wall to turn on the washer," directed Hammett as he lay a slab of yellow cheese between two pieces of bread, then slapped it into the skillet to toast.

Holbrook tied on a greasy white apron and set to work on the dishes. It all worked pretty much as it did at Irving's place, but the round metal dishwasher was bigger.

While he worked, a black-haired toy poodle kept bursting in and out of the kitchen, bringing in tubs of dirty plates, grabbing new plates loaded with food, and shouting out new orders.

"Fries and eggs. Over easy, no salt. Make the fries crispy."

Hammett would nod and add another skillet to

his line of dancing gas burners, then settle a basket of white fries into a vat of bubbling grease with a satisfying sizzle.

Holbrook swallowed hungrily and tried to concentrate on the dishes. His arms trembled and his head swam. He hoped he wouldn't faint. He'd never been so hungry in his life!

Hammett flipped another cheese sandwich in one of his skillets. It was perfectly toasted. Cheese oozed from the sides, and the edge of the cheese was brown and crispy. He slipped the sandwich onto a plate and held it out to Holbrook.

"Here," he said.

The dishes weren't done, but Holbrook eagerly tore off his apron and grabbed the plate.

"Just a minute," Hammett snatched back the plate, then added a heap of hot fries.

Holbrook hurried into the alley and gratefully bit into the sandwich. It was the best grilled-cheese sandwich he had ever had. It was gone in three bites. Then he tackled the fries. He'd had only a few when the three pigeons sidled up to him.

"Crumbs for the poor?" cooed One Leg.

"I earned this," said Holbrook. "I've been working. Go away."

It seemed that everyone in the city wanted things from him!

Holbrook bit into a fry. Crispy on the outside, soft and hot on the inside. Just the way he liked it.

Scabs bent her head low; her eyes were flat and

tired. Lone Eye turned away and hunched his shoulders. One Leg tried to look as if he didn't care. Suddenly, Holbrook found it hard to swallow.

He set down the plate. "Here."

The three pigeons eagerly pecked up his leftover fries, now totally ignoring him.

"You could at least say thank you," protested Holbrook.

"Bless you," mumbled Scabs. She was barely able to speak, her beak was so crammed.

One Leg yawned, then thrust a second leg out from under his feathers and scratched himself. He wasn't one legged at all! He saw Holbrook staring and shrugged sheepishly. "A fellow's got to make a living."

"So what happened to your stuff?" asked Lone Eye.

And Holbrook suddenly remembered the factory and the other animals. Without answering Lone Eye, he hurried back into the kitchen.

19

"Mr. Hammett?" Holbrook said. He didn't want to disturb the busy cook, but he *had* to get someone's help.

"Just Hammett," said the bulldog, not taking his eyes off his sizzling skillets.

Suddenly, Holbrook realized how hard it was going to be to explain about the factory and everything.

Even so, he plunged in, telling about the animals and how they were trapped and had to paint all the time just to pay for their food and a place to sleep, but they could never pay it off. Hammett frowned, but when Holbrook mentioned who owned the factory, he stopped his cooking and turned to stare at him. "Count Rumolde?" he asked.

Holbrook nodded.

The bulldog barked out a laugh. "How long did you say you've been in the city?" he asked.

Holbrook counted on his fingers. It was hard to believe it had been only four days.

"Count Rumolde is one of the most respected animals of the city," said Hammett.

"But the animals are practically slaves," said Holbrook.

"You say he feeds them and gives them a place to live, right?"

Holbrook nodded.

"Artists," Hammett shook his head. "I know all about them. A lot of artists live around here, and they like things for free. It doesn't work that way." He turned back to his burners.

"But, it's different—" Holbrook stopped. Hammett wasn't listening anymore. He simply didn't believe him and never would. Holbrook wondered if anyone would believe him.

He thought of Margot Frogtayne and Enrico Escargot. They might believe him, but he had no idea how to reach them. And *would* they believe him? Rumolde had been right; it was Holbrook's word against the count's.

Still, it was worth a try. Margot and Enrico would be at the Exhibition. But how would he get in? He remembered how Squeak took the applications and guarded the door. Holbrook frowned. It seemed that the count was everywhere he turned.

Later that afternoon, after the dirty dishes had finally stopped coming, Holbrook was able to take another break.

Hammett gave him some scrambled eggs and

more fries. "Good work," he said. "Be ready for the dinner rush."

Holbrook nodded, then went outside and settled on the back stoop. The instant he did, the pigeons fluttered up, cooing eagerly. He shoved his plate toward them.

He wasn't hungry anyway. All afternoon he had been thinking about the animals in the factory and what a fool he had been.

He thought about how easily Rumolde had convinced him that he *was* extraordinary. The talk of the town! Holbrook blushed. What a failure he had turned out to be. He didn't even have *Starry Sky* anymore. All that was left of Holbrook the great artist were hundreds of *Desert Sunsets* stacked up like so many boards in Rumolde's basement.

But maybe he *could* do one great thing. He could free the other artists.

He just had to!

He glanced at the pigeons. One Leg was contentedly pecking at his feathers now that his stomach was full.

What if someone *else* entered the competition and got into the hall to talk to Margot and Enrico?

"Do you do anything?" Holbrook asked One Leg. "I mean, besides beg?"

One Leg looked a little offended. "We have many adventures," he announced.

"Once a squirrel gave me an entire sandwich," said Scabs, nodding in agreement.

90

"I found a brand-new shoe in a Dumpster," said Lone Eye. "It was a leftie, as I recall."

"No—I mean, like sing or dance or draw?"

The pigeons glanced at each other.

"Once I kept a blue jay up all night with my cooing," announced Lone Eye. "He threw a shoe at me. It was a rightie, as I recall. If I'd still had the leftie, I would have had two shoes."

Holbrook sighed. He didn't think the Artiste Exhibition Extraordinaire was looking for someone with a knack for finding shoes.

Then he had a thought. He was a nobody. The pigeons were nobodies. What if the pigeons took a painting to the Exhibition? No one would know if they had painted it or not. Holbrook glanced about. The first thing he needed to do was get paints and a canvas and brushes. But how?

"That's nothing," One Leg was saying, bragging to Lone Eye. "I once found a silk cravat. It only had one small ketchup stain. I looked quite handsome in it."

That was it! Holbrook stood up excitedly. What could *he* find in the garbage? Hammett had said a lot of artists lived in the area. What had they discarded?

20

Holbrook had never gone through garbage cans or Dumpsters before. He was amazed at what creatures threw out. Along with wilted lettuce, half-eaten apples, and melon rinds were books and baby carriages, dinner plates and hats—someone had even put an old sofa in the alley.

The pigeons didn't seem surprised.

"It's a wasteful world," said Lone Eye.

"These are perhaps offerings to the gods," said One Leg, who seemed to have grown quite grand now that Holbrook had explained about how they would go to the Exhibition and enter Holbrook's painting as if it were theirs.

"If you can pretend you're an artist, that is," Holbrook had said.

"Pretend I'm an artist?" said One Leg. "You forget that I have fooled some of the finest creatures in this city with my one leg. I am a master of deception."

Scabs and Lone Eye had also been eager to help,

especially after Holbrook told them about the factory and how they needed to tell Margot and Enrico.

"I know about prison bars," Lone Eye had announced, but he didn't elaborate.

Scabs hadn't said anything, but she immediately began pecking through Dumpsters. Now Holbrook noticed that she kept glancing toward an alcove near one of them. There, propped against the wall, but obviously discarded, was a half-finished painting. He snatched it up. He could turn the canvas around and use the back.

In a garbage can farther down the alley, he found a brush. It was missing half its bristles, but those that remained were of the finest sable. Now all he needed was some paint.

The three pigeons settled on the old sofa and directed him to promising-looking garbage cans.

But although Holbrook did find some tubes of paint, they had been squeezed empty.

"Perhaps you could buy some," said One Leg. "There's an art supply store just a few blocks away."

Holbrook wondered if Hammett would give him some money, but he had the feeling his food and the cot in the back room that Hammett had shown him were his pay for now.

Suddenly, he realized that Scabs was holding a quarter in her claws.

"Where'd you get that?" he asked.

She shrugged but glanced down at the sofa.

The pigeons squawked when Holbrook shooed

them off. Fishing about under the cushions and in the cracks, he came up with a fistful of coins. Maybe it would be enough.

The store was busy, but hushed, and Holbrook realized that there was a lot of quiet thinking going on. Animals of all types carefully studied pencils and pens and paints and paper. His heart quickened. Here were creatures like himself, lost in dreams of the wonderful things they could make.

Feeling rather shy, he stood quietly next to an opossum who was squinting at a giant bank of paint tubes.

Never had he seen so many colors to choose from. The names sent his imagination soaring.

Alizarin crimson, cerulean blue, burnt umber, vermillion, dove gray, tourmaline green, king's blue, lampblack. There were even colors made from real gold and copper and silver.

But he didn't have much money. He studied the prices carefully, then bought the only two tubes he could afford—black and white.

Holbrook returned to the alley behind Hammett's café. He undid the canvas on the old painting, turned it around, and tacked it back on the stretcher bars. It was a little lumpy, but it would have to do. He propped the canvas on top of a box, where he also laid out his two colors, his brush, and a jar of water. It wasn't much, but it was enough. It seemed like a long time since he had painted. He sighed happily and looked around.

Now, what should he paint?

21

The city was so different from the desert. In the desert, things stood silent and single and still. In the city, there was only noise, numbers, and ceaseless movement. Perhaps he could make an important statement about the city. He considered the nearby Dumpster, spilling garbage and rotten smells. He could say the city was rotten and perhaps paint a picture of hard shadows and garbage, but his heart wasn't really in it.

He eyed One Leg, who pecked nearby, glancing curiously at Holbrook's setup. Holbrook had never done a portrait before. In the desert, he painted distant things.

"How would you like to pose for me?" Holbrook asked.

"Pose for you?" One Leg asked uncertainly.

"All you have to do is stand there," said Holbrook.

"What's in it for me?"

"I gave you fries, didn't I?" said Holbrook. He'd

been feeding One Leg all his leftovers and this was the thanks he got?

"But you gave me those already. I don't have to do anything," the pigeon pointed out.

"Well, then, here's your chance to earn them!"

"Then you will no longer be generous and good," persisted One Leg. "Ours will be a business arrangement."

Holbrook scowled. One Leg pecked rather smugly at his breast feathers.

"Here's *your* chance to be generous," Holbrook announced. "You will no longer be a phony two-legged beggar, but a creature with something to give."

This idea seemed to be a novelty for One Leg, and at last he agreed.

Holbrook had him stand against the brick wall of the restaurant. "And put your leg back up. I want you with one leg."

"But that's a lie. Phony—you said so yourself."

"Art is about truth, but it doesn't have to be real," said Holbrook grandly, not really sure if that was right. But it sounded as if it might be.

One Leg gave him a look but tucked his left leg into his feathers and stood patiently while Holbrook painted.

As it sometimes did when things went right, a sort of magic happened as Holbrook worked. There was something about One Leg, something he wanted to show. He wasn't quite sure what it was, but he kept mixing different grays and shifting shapes and changing brush strokes until he felt he had it.

At last, he stepped back from the canvas, and One Leg eagerly came around to see.

"That's me?" the pigeon said after a moment.

At the bottom of the canvas was something that looked a bit like a one-legged pigeon standing stiff and worn, but the rest of the picture was filled with shapes, like wings that seemed to shimmer above One Leg.

"What's this squiggle?" One Leg pointed at an odd blotch shivering on one edge of the canvas.

Holbrook grabbed the painting. Squiggles again! He might as well paint desert sunsets and calendar cactuses for the rest of his life!

"Now, now," said One Leg, "I'm not saying I don't like it. Although I do think I have a few more feathers than you show. But this part," he waved at the shimmering wing shapes, "this part is nice. It makes me feel special somehow. Perhaps I *am* the King of Pigeons merely disguised as a beggar."

He cackled, then called the others over to see. Scabs turned her head to look at it with one eye and then the other. Lone Eye gazed at it unblinking.

"It is a fine likeness," announced Lone Eye.

"Yes," agreed Scabs.

Holbrook liked it, too. It was a real painting. And he realized that he could paint many more pictures. The thing inside was bigger than just one painting. Maybe some day he'd do something even better than *Starry Sky!*

"You may call me Your Highness," One Leg instruced the others. "King of Pigeonia."

Holbrook laughed, then thought of Count Rumolde. Maybe he wasn't a real count, either. All you had to do was look well fed and sound important, and creatures would believe anything. Especially if you had a lot of money.

Then Holbrook felt his throat beating. Suddenly, he had an even better idea about how to rescue the animals in the factory. Even better than hoping to have the pigeons talk to Margot and Enrico. He had an idea about how he might free his friends right away!

22

"They'll never let us in," said Lone Eye.

The pigeons and Holbrook peered around the edge of the Mordred Arms at the red-coated bullfrog who guarded the front doors.

"Of course they will," said Holbrook, not feeling at all sure. "He's the King of Pigeons."

One Leg did indeed look fine. His feathers were glossy with preening and a little French fry grease. Even though it wasn't raining, he held a small purple umbrella. It was from a Dumpster, but they'd straightened out the one bent spoke. It was a shiny silk and gave One Leg an exotic, important air.

Lone Eye and Scabs stood on either side of him, looking like bodyguards or servants. Scabs carried a small black briefcase (another Dumpster find), and it clinked when she moved, as if stuffed with coins.

"We shall proceed," declared One Leg.

And the three pigeons headed for the door. As they'd rehearsed, Lone Eye announced fiercely,

"Make way for the King of Pigeons. Make way!"

The bullfrog saw them coming, stared for a moment, then snapped to attention.

He bowed and flung open the door. One Leg swept into the building as if he truly were a king.

"Welcome, Your Highness," the doorman croaked.

Holbrook scurried in after them. The bullfrog apparently remembered him from before and waved him on in. But once in the lobby, Holbrook crouched low and scuttled toward the door to the basement.

No one was paying any attention to him. All eyes were on One Leg, the King of Pigeons.

"Is Count Rumolde in?" demanded Lone Eye of the manager. "The King of Pigeons is here to see him."

The cockatoo bobbed his head nervously and snapped a claw at a mouse behind the counter, who quickly lifted up the phone and placed a call.

"Tell him," said One Leg, "tell him that I wish to purchase a staggering amount of art for the many palaces and lodges and habitations in my kingdom."

As quickly as the pigeons could gobble down fries, Count Rumolde descended from his penthouse apartment, and emerged from his gilded elevator with Squeak in tow. Brushing back the golden streak in his fur, he strode toward One Leg, a gleaming smile on his snout.

"Your Excellency," he said. "Welcome to my humble abode."

"Count," cooed One Leg. "It is a pleasure."

One Leg had folded up his umbrella and now used it like a cane. He stabbed at the air with it to emphasize his points.

"My minions tell me that you can supply me with untold art treasures for my kingdom." Stab, stab. "My minions tell me that *you* put the 'art' in 'artifice.'" Stab.

Rumolde frowned.

"Oh, dear, English is not my native tongue. Perhaps I misspoke?" One Leg gazed blandly about him. "But I hope my intentions are clear. I need art, and I'm prepared to pay handsomely for it."

Scabs set down the black briefcase with a thump. It was clearly very heavy.

"I particularly like kittens," said One Leg. "And autumn leaves. And spring leaves, too. Do you think you might be able to help me?"

Rumolde's smile returned. "I think I can be of service. How many pieces would you like?"

"All of it."

"All?"

"Every piece you've got, my dear count. Every scrap, every tatter. But I should warn you, I'm in a hurry. I'd like to take it all now. As much as you can give me, if you please."

Rumolde's eyes widened, and he leaned over to whisper in Squeak's ear. Squeak hurried to the phone and placed a call.

Soon Holbrook, crouched behind one of the lobby chairs, heard the tramp of paws coming up the stairs from the basement. The door opened, and out came the guards from the factory, staggering under stacks of paintings, as many as they could carry.

Just as Holbrook had hoped, Rumolde in his greed had emptied the room of guards so they could carry up the art.

The animals in the lobby all stared in surprise. Holbrook wondered if they had any idea of the real source of Count Rumolde's wealth.

One Leg murmured his approval and began to study each painting.

"Ah, the brush strokes! The color! Although it could perhaps use a bit of red," he murmured, looking at one of the mouse's meadows. "Please, I'd like a closer look."

And he urged the guards to bring the paintings to him for closer inspection. With any luck, One Leg would keep them all busy for a long time.

As the last of the guards hustled through the basement door, Holbrook quietly slipped inside. With the guards out of the way, he could let the factory animals out.

He hurried down the stairs and through the maze of corridors. He was pretty sure he remembered the way. He turned right, left, right, left. There was the factory door. He reached for the knob. But before he could turn it, a paw clamped down on his.

"We've been waiting for you," Frick snarled.

23

To Holbrook's surprise, rather than taking him back to the factory, Frick marched him down the hall to a simple wooden door.

Behind it, dimly lit stairs led down to an even lower level in the building.

"Come on. Get a move on," said Frick, herding him down the steps.

At the bottom was a large prison cell. Enrico Escargot and Margot Frogtayne rushed up to him from behind the bars. What were *they* doing here?

Frick shoved Holbrook into the cell and slammed the barred door shut with a clang.

Behind Enrico was his entire opera troupe!

"What's going on?" Holbrook cried.

But before they could answer, Homarus Cray Lobster, the art critic from Rumolde's party, spoke from atop a nearby crate. He held his spectacles up to his eyes to better peer down at Holbrook. "We are obviously in a prison cell." The lobster waved a claw

around the room. "As to the purpose of our imprisonment, I can only conjecture."

"Rumolde invited us to dinner last night," said Enrico. "But as soon as we stepped into his penthouse, his servants grabbed us and brought us down here. My troupe was already here—lured down earlier, I'm afraid, by the promise of wine and song."

Several of the snails hung their heads.

"We could not resist," admitted one. "They do say the count has the finest wine cellar in the city."

"He is a beast," said Margot. "A barbarian!"

A large goose waddled up, gabbling excitedly. "I'm sure he won't hurt us. He couldn't. He's an art lover. Count Rumolde is a connoisseur," the goose honked. "A man of refinement. He's read all my poems."

The lobster, shaking his head rather sadly at the goose, muttered, "This is Miss Gosling, the popular poetess."

The way he said "popular" made Holbrook think that the lobster didn't think much of Miss Gosling's poetry.

"Art is for everyone, not just eggheads like yourself," Miss Gosling said, thrusting her beak into the air.

Just then the door above opened, and they all watched as Maurice, the orangutan chef, made his way down the stairs with sighs and groans. His belly was round and heavy. His jaw thrust out in annoyance. "I am not an acrobat," the ape complained. "I am a chef. Not a contortionist. Not a circus performer. A chef."

He lumbered down the last step, then stood studying them, mopping his brow with his soiled chef's hat.

Frick followed close behind carrying a large silver tray covered with a silver dome. And behind him came Rumolde, looking very angry.

When the mink reached the bottom, he glared and pointed at Holbrook. "I am not amused by your trick with the pigeons," he said.

"Pigeons?" asked Margot.

"The King of Pigeons," said Holbrook, and he couldn't help smiling at the thought of what must have been the expression on Rumolde's face when he discovered the briefcase was full of old bricks and stones.

"They made their escape," said Rumolde. "Otherwise, I would add pigeon pie to my menu."

"Menu?" said Miss Gosling.

Holbrook did not like the way the chef was examining them. "Finally, something to work with!" said the ape. "Enough of beans and Jell-O blobs."

His tiny eyes landed on Holbrook. "Does he have to be included? There's nothing you can do with a lizard!"

"He is one of the most important," said the mink. "I must have him."

"Count Rumolde," Enrico said, stepping forward. "What are your intentions?"

"We are clearly political prisoners, probably because of my recent article in the *Splitting Hairs Review,*" announced the lobster from his perch on top of the crate.

"You are among the greatest artists in the world," said Rumolde, as if that explained things. "Except the goose, of course. I just happen to like foie gras."

"Foie gras?" asked Holbrook.

"Goose liver," whispered one of the snails.

"*What* about my liver?" honked Miss Gosling.

Ignoring her, Rumolde pointed at Homarus. "Of course, you're not an artist, either. Still, as an art critic, you will add a piquant flavor to my feast."

"Feast?" cried Enrico.

"Yes, you will be cooked quite exquisitely by my master chef." Maurice beamed. "And then . . . I will eat you," Rumolde said, as if it were the most natural thing in the world.

There was a shocked silence. Eaten? Sometimes there were rumors of predator animals going wild. But in the cities and towns, for one animal to deliberately kill and eat another? It was unheard of.

"That can't be," said Holbrook. "Why would you want to eat us?"

"Because *you've* got it and *I* don't!" snarled Rumolde, suddenly savage. "You can do it! And I can only pretend."

Holbrook remembered how the mink had shouted and grabbed at him in the art studio, but he still didn't understand. What was this "it" he kept talking about?

But then, as before, Rumolde seemed to remember himself and, after a few deep breaths, added in a calm, explaining sort of tone, "I could be a great artist. But I've been thwarted for years. I lack one little thing." Rumolde ran a tense paw over his golden streak. "Talent.

"That's where you come in. You are all loaded with talent. I will consume you and your talent along with you. With each bite, my talent will grow. And then I will be the greatest artist in the world!"

"That's madness!" cried Enrico.

Miss Gosling swooned.

The other animals cried out, but Rumolde paid no attention.

"Also, it eliminates a bit of competition," he noted to no one in particular.

"Now, then, Maurice," he said to the ape. "As I promised, here are your ingredients. The finest ingredients in the world, in fact! Let's see what you can do. I will be ready to dine tomorrow following the Exhibition. Although I will dine alone, I do believe it will be a victory celebration."

With that, Rumolde leapt back up the stairs—on all fours, like the beast he was.

Maurice waved his long brown fingers at the weasel. "Frick, serve them. We must keep them plump."

With a scowl, Frick lifted the dome off the tray and slid the tray through an opening in the cell door.

On the tray were five smaller platters.

There was a cream puff dribbled with chocolate for Margot, a thick slice of apple pie for Miss Gosling, a cup of fine sea broth for Homarus, and pasta glistening with creamy sauce for Enrico and his troupe. For Holbrook there was a plate of beans.

"That's all there was for you," grumbled Maurice waving at Holbrook's beans. "You see what I have had to put up with? The greatest chef in the world. I am not a hash slinger. I am not a short-order cook. I am a—"

Then he stopped as if struck by a thought.

"Sherry," he said, pointing a bent finger at Holbrook. "Lightly poached in sherry with perhaps a touch of fennel. Yes. Yes! That will do."

He lumbered back up the stairs, helping to hoist himself with his long hairy arms, muttering recipes to himself.

Frick's tongue darted over his thin lips.

"Dibs on the leftovers," he announced as he slipped up the stairs behind the chef.

24

"Eaten?" whispered one of the snails as Frick slunk away. She began to weep.

Margot hurried over to comfort her.

Miss Gosling staggered forward, recovered from her swoon. She stared at her plate then announced, "We must keep up our strength," and began gobbling her pie.

Looking over at the others, she slowed her gobbling, then finally stopped with a gulp.

"What's wrong?" she whispered. "Is it poisoned?"

"We will not eat the food of our captors," said Margot with a defiant toss of her head.

"Yes, indeed," said Homarus. "Why, this is just like *The Count of Monte Cristo*. I must find a pen and begin my prison memoirs."

"Maybe we can escape," said Holbrook.

"Don't trouble yourself," said Homarus. "We've already looked. There is no escape."

But Holbrook explored the cell, anyway. He

found only solid cement walls. The sturdy bars in front were covered with a fine steely mesh. Not even the snails could crawl out.

"We are hors d'oeuvres!" one cried.

"He can't mean to eat us," said Miss Gosling. "He—he's joking!"

"It is a well-known custom in primitive cultures," lectured Homarus. "The warrior believes that if he consumes the heart of his enemy, he will acquire his enemy's courage and daring. Rumolde apparently believes he will acquire our talent."

"Well, I think it sounds silly," honked Miss Gosling.

"It's madness!" said Enrico. "He's mad with jealousy. It doesn't matter if it's true or not. He believes it. He will do as he says."

Margot gazed sadly at her long legs.

"Will I never dance again?" she said. "Will no one see my lovely leaps and turns?"

"My beautiful songs," sighed Enrico. "I have so many songs yet to sing."

Holbrook stared at the gray walls and floor. He still had so many paintings inside, too! He wondered what he would paint if he had a canvas here now.

Then he looked up at Margot. "Maybe you *could* dance again, Margot. Here. It would just be us, but—"

"*Mais oui!*" she cried. "But of course! We must have an evening of art. One last performance for all of us."

"Yes! That's it," cried the other animals.

And in no time at all they had rearranged several of the crates in a circle to make a tiny stage.

"Now, who will go first?" asked Enrico.

There was a rustling in the back and the faint clearing of a throat.

"Miss Gosling?" asked Enrico.

"If you insist." The goose quickly waddled to center stage. "I shall recite from my greatest work," she said. *"The Barnyard and Other Sorrows."*

"The other sorrows being all the rest of the poems in the book," muttered Homarus.

Miss Gosling ignored him. She raised her beak skyward and suddenly honked,

"i wake
i lie
i lie awake

"i cry
i laugh
i ask why"

Here she paused, her head held high:

"i die"

Miss Gosling dropped her head upon her breast.

"Dare I eat a ladybug?" she suddenly cried, raising her head, again.

"i have measured out my life in mealy worms
eating the worms who will one day eat me
i grow old, i grow old
i shall have to get my hair rolled."

There was a long silence. Then the animals
clapped politely.

Miss Gosling offered to recite another, but
Homarus scuttled onto the stage and shooed her
away with his feelers.

"While Miss Gosling was reciting, I was able to jot
down a few words for my upcoming prison memoir.
I will share them with you now." Waving his spectacles in one claw and a scrap of paper in the other,
Homarus Cray Lobster began, "The soul grows damp
and despondent in this place of perpetual night. The
cries of the other animals are saddening, but I keep to
myself, retaining my strength. I must survive, I tell
myself. I must live to tell the world."

He stopped.

"Eez that all?" asked Margot.

"One can *imagine* the possibilities," said Homarus,
rather stiffly.

"I'm sure it will be wonderful," said Enrico, giving the nod to his troupe.

The snails rushed the stage, pushing Homarus
aside, and launched into a dark lament from *Twilight
of the Mollusks.*

At the conclusion, Enrico beamed with pride
and then, bowing in Margot's direction, said, "Now

perhaps Mademoiselle Frogtayne would do us the honor?"

Margot bowed in return. She straightened and for just a moment held them all quiet with the still grace of her pose. Then, she began to dance.

Holbrook had never seen anything so beautiful. She moved over the cement floor of the cell as if floating. Her hands were as graceful as petals. She leapt so high, the other animals gasped. The dance seemed to tell a story of moving free and strong. Holbrook blinked. It felt as if he had desert sand in his eyes, but he knew that wasn't the reason for his tears.

When it was over, Margot flung back her head, flushed and defiant. "Now you, Enrico," she said. "Sing us your finest song."

"I will sing from a great opera by Piggini. It is the story of a snail who is imprisoned and about to be executed. He sings of the beautiful snail he adores and the life he loves."

Enrico perched on a crate and began. "*E lucevan le stelle,* the stars were shining," he sang, his voice slow and soft. But it grew with the song and soon filled the cell, the basement, the city, maybe the whole world.

"I die despairing," he cried, and then his voice fell again as the song of loss ended. "Yet never before have I loved life so much."

There were cheers and stomping feet. Homarus was beside himself. "This is the greatest night in art history. We have given the performances of our lives!" he cried.

"What about him," honked Miss Gosling, pointing her beak at Holbrook. "He hasn't done anything."

"But he has no paints. What can he do?" said Margot.

"Here," said Holbrook.

He grabbed a dusty board that was propped against a wall, studied it for a moment, then quickly sketched in the dust with his finger.

"It's just a bunch of lines," complained the goose.

"It's Mademoiselle Frogtayne," said Homarus. "One can easily see the grace, the power. It's her dancing."

"Eez it, Holbrook?" asked Margot.

Holbrook nodded shyly.

"Thank you. It eez lovely," she said, and leaning forward she kissed him quickly on the cheek.

Holbrook's heart soared, and he thought it was perhaps worth being in the prison cell, worth facing death, for Margot's kiss. But later that night, when he awoke from a restless sleep, his stomach tightened with an awful fear.

Across from the cell was an open door—leading to a room he hadn't seen before. He could see the cement walls and stone floor and a large white sink and giant butcher block. The block was worn and gouged. Maurice was in there, hunched over a spinning stone wheel, and Holbrook could hear the

116

viscous whir, the steely whisper of a knife being sharpened.

Holbrook suddenly realized that this place was "there." The "there" that all the animals feared so much. He curled up tight on the cold floor, closed his eyes, and waited.

25

"Get the lizard first. His meat is the toughest. He will take the longest."

Holbrook knew that Maurice and Frick had been studying them for a while, but he had laid unmoving, with his eyes closed. He was to be the first taken, and that was what he had hoped to hear. Earlier he had deliberately moved to the very front of the cell. He had a plan.

The cell door creaked open. Holbrook sensed Frick bending down, felt the weasel's crawly whiskers on his cheek and his thin fingers slip under his shoulders. That's when Holbrook exploded.

He sprang for Frick's face, scratching and snarling. The weasel screamed in pain and tried to push him away.

Then Miss Gosling attacked. She must have been thinking the same thing as Holbrook. At least they would put up a fight! She lunged at Maurice, hissing hysterically. She snapped and jabbed at Maurice's legs with her powerful beak. When Maurice kicked at her, she flew at him. Her wings were like a rush of wind.

Homarus rushed forward snapping with his large red claws.

"Run!" cried Holbrook. "Everybody run for it."

Even snails can move fairly quickly, if necessary.

But it was too late. Maurice quietly raised his long arm. Margot hung by her legs from his fist.

She trembled. Her proud eyes were wide with fear and horror.

"She will be the first," said Maurice, waving her at Holbrook. "Unless you come quietly."

Margot twisted in his grasp.

"I'll come quietly," Holbrook said. "Put her down."

Maurice set Margot down carefully, but not before studying her plump legs with interest. "I have it," he said snapping his fingers. "Frog legs amidst a parsley puree."

Margot sank to the cell floor, her fine head bent low.

The weasel bared his teeth at Miss Gosling, but she had already retreated into a corner. No one wanted to see Margot hurt.

The prisoners were herded back into the cell and the door locked.

"You will die quickly and painlessly—if you cooperate," said Maurice. "My knives are sharp. Otherwise, there are other methods . . . like boiling water," he added, staring at Homarus, who also tried to look brave but whose feelers trembled violently.

Maurice shoved Holbrook toward the little back room. The chef's leathery palm was soft, but his hand was as big as Holbrook's back and strong.

Holbrook stumbled forward. Just before he entered the room, he glanced back. His heart was pounding with fear, but suddenly, oddly, at this most awful moment, he felt he had never before seen the things of the world so clearly. Even in the gloom of the prison, the black of Miss Gosling's eyes gleamed and Margot's bent body was as graceful as tender stalk of grass. The dust motes caught in a shaft of light were scattered gold—as beautiful as stars.

Funny how he had never noticed before. Funny how he had never noticed so many things before. He blinked back sudden tears. He would never paint this. He would never paint anything again.

Then Maurice shoved him toward the white sink and the scarred butcher block. Frick slithered in behind them, his eye glinting hungrily.

The ape plucked Holbrook up and laid him on his back, pinning him with a heavy hand. Holbrook's eyes darted anxiously about. The block was stained with dark splotches he knew must be old blood. He could smell it. Metallic and rank.

Holbrook thought his heart might stop with fear. Above its pounding, he heard Maurice humming softly to himself.

The chef studied his gleaming knives, reaching

first for one, then pausing and reaching for another. Holbrook saw a look of thoughtful contentment and yet excitement on the ape's face. He suddenly realized he knew that look. It was like that of the artists at the store as they studied the paints and brushes.

Maurice thought he was an artist! Like them! Holbrook couldn't believe it. He couldn't believe the ape had that same feeling. How could *he* be big inside? He was fat and crazy and not like Holbrook at all.

And then Holbrook remembered Jagger, the horned lizard, running up to him and giving him the paintbrush he had taken. Jagger, who made fun of him and called his paintings squiggles. He suddenly knew why Jagger had his paintbrush.

Holbrook swallowed. He had to do this just right. Even though he tried to keep his voice steady, it squeaked as he said, "It's too bad only Rumolde will get to taste us. Such a fine meal."

Maurice frowned slightly. He eased up the pressure of his hand, just a bit. He ran his eyes thoughtfully over Holbrook's body. Probably thinking of the best way to slice him up, Holbrook thought.

"What do you have in mind?" Holbrook asked, trying to sound casual. As if the recipe weren't himself! "For me, I mean. How do you plan to cook me?"

"Ahh," Maurice's eyes lit up. "I rejected the fennel idea. You are not fancy. You are not fine. Then it came to me—the pungent smell of sage. I will evoke your desert origins. I found some fresh at the market."

"Sage? Desert origins? What are you talking

about?" interrupted Frick, impatiently. "Let's get on with it."

Maurice angrily pulled on his lip, and Holbrook spoke quickly. "Maurice is an artist. Can't you see that? He is a famous chef. The recipes he chooses are important."

"He slings hash," muttered Frick.

Maurice swiped at him with his hairy arm, but Frick danced out of reach. "I'll have you know that once I had my own restaurant. My creations were the talk of the culinary world."

"Yeah, well . . ." Frick eyed Maurice's grubby apron.

"No one understood," said Holbrook, cautiously sitting up. "No one appreciated your greatness."

Maurice nodded; his small eyes grew a bit moist.

"And now, such a waste. Such a pity," said Holbrook. "Your greatest achievement . . . and only the mink will know."

"Cut his throat!" the weasel snarled.

Maurice glared at him but reached for a knife.

"Of course, there *is* a way all the world could know of your greatness," Holbrook said quickly. "But Rumolde would never allow it."

"What won't he allow?" said Maurice. "I do what I wish with my creations."

"Yes, the ordinary ones. The ones for the stomach."

"What other kind is there?" scoffed the chef, raising a thin, sharp blade.

"Any chef can cook for the stomach," Holbrook said hurriedly. "But you are bigger than that."

Maurice glanced down at his belly, looking puzzled.

Holbrook quickly explained. "If you kill us, only Rumolde will know of your feast. It will be a small thing, quickly gone. Let us live, and you will be the talk of the Exhibition. The talk of Golden City. The talk of the world!"

Holbrook scrambled to his feet. "Imagine the most unusual meal in the world, where the food lives and actually entertains the guests!"

He held up his paws and spread them out, as if imagining a banner. "Using the greatest artists in the world, Maurice LeMonde creates food for the very soul!"

"You're supposed to cook them for the count!" cried Frick.

"Yes, of course. Rumolde. I forgot," said Holbrook, glancing at the chef who was beginning to tremble with suppressed emotion. "Of course, you must do as Rumolde says. Just like all his servants. Just like—"

"I am not a servant!" Maurice suddenly roared. "I am not a lackey. I am not a worm to operate in obscurity. I am the world's greatest chef, and all the world shall know!"

"I'm telling!" Frick turned to run, but Maurice grabbed him.

"No, you don't. You can wait in the prison cell."

He pointed a pudgy finger at Holbrook. "You. Free the others. We must plan the feast!"

26

Count Rumolde moved easily through the bustling crowd at the Artiste Exhibition Extraordinaire. He nodded and smiled graciously at the many animals who rushed forward to congratulate him on his entry.

"It is a masterpiece," gushed the Duchess of Woof. "When I look at it, I feel the grandness of the stars and the sky."

"I am not surprised that it should speak to someone of your fine sensibilities," he said smoothly, coming to a stop next to Holbrook's *Starry Sky*.

The painting was in a thick gold frame, and the sign beneath it read: *Starry Sky*. Acrylic on Canvas. By Count Rainier Rumolde.

"It speaks to all," trumpeted Ms. Swanson.

Corvus Cawfield and Andy Wartsnall stopped before it. The crow and the hedgehog studied it, then gave each other quiet nods of approval.

Rumolde's eyes glowed with a deep fire of satisfaction. But suddenly he frowned.

Maurice was wheeling a big dining cart into the hall. All around him animals fell back with murmurs of disbelief and shock.

Laid out on the cart were animal carcasses displayed as a feast! A whole goose and a lobster formed the centerpiece; the goose's white neck curved gracefully around the glistening red claw of the lobster. To the side was a plate of escargots—snails— decorated with fresh herbs and flowers. A pair of lovely green frog legs peeked out from a bed of parsley. Off to one side was a platter covered with a large silver dome.

Rumolde strode up to Maurice.

"What are you doing here?" he muttered. "I told you I would have my meal after the Exhibition!"

"A meal for you alone," said Maurice.

"Of course," said Rumolde in a low voice, revealing his sharp teeth in a fake smile to the crowd. "What are you thinking!"

"Do you know this creature?" demanded Corvus Cawfield.

Rumolde straightened and addressed the crowd loudly, "He's mad but harmless. Don't worry, he's under my control."

Maurice trembled with rage. "I am not a mindless tool. I am not a barbarian. I am not a destroyer," he declared with a joyful shout. "I am a creator. I—I am *an artist!*"

The crowd awoke from its shock, and outraged voices rose about him.

Ignoring them, Maurice waved grandly at the cart. "I present to you the greatest meal ever prepared. I present to you . . . a feast for the very soul!"

And one by one the angry voices fell silent. Rising above the shouts was a small, clear voice singing a beautiful tune.

And then other voices joined in, and suddenly those watching realized that the plate of snails had begun to move. They reared up, singing in chorus, and from the very center arose the great Enrico Escargot, his strong tenor voice ringing out in a song of joyous celebration. All the beautifully arranged dishes on the table began to stir. With a gasp, the crowd realized that the banquet before them was alive!

"Look! It's Margot Frogtayne!" cried an onlooker as Margot leapt from her bed of parsley.

With a dazzling pirouette, she whirled to the center of the table and began to dance, performing leaps and turns that made the crowd roar.

She was spectacular, but Holbrook, who had slipped down from the cart to watch, secretly thought that her dance in the prison cell the night before had been more beautiful.

All the animals had something to offer in this great performance. Miss Gosling recited several poems; Homarus gave a speech, which was promptly interrupted by cries from the crowd for another song from Enrico. Then, as Enrico's song ended, Miss Gosling gave the cart several hard thrusts with her beak and sent it sliding across the floor. She scrambled after it as all the performers bowed. The animals disappeared through a nearby door to the wild claps and hoots of the crowd.

27

As the cart disappeared, Rumolde quickly stepped forward and began to speak. "Bravo, Maurice! A triumph—just as I'd told you it would be. Congratulations!"

The ape stared at the mink, his mouth hanging down in surprise.

"What are you talking about?" said Holbrook, the only one of the group left behind. "You planned to eat us!"

"Eat you! Why, you obviously completely misunderstood," declared the mink smiling warmly and reaching out toward Holbrook.

Holbrook dodged his grasp.

"Maurice and I discussed this very idea—a living feast. I told him it was brilliant. I told him I would become his patron, providing him with the finest ingredients—vegetarian, of course—for his very own restaurant, because surely he is the greatest chef in the world. Isn't that so, Maurice?"

Maurice narrowed his eyes but nodded his head. He had always dreamed of owning another restaurant and reclaiming his reputation.

Holbrook couldn't believe it! His heart pounded with anger and fear. Then suddenly he spotted *Starry Sky*. It took him a second to realize what it was. He'd never seen his art like that—in a big frame, looking like a real painting in a real museum. But then he saw the sign with Rumolde's name on it.

"And look," Holbrook cried. "He's stolen my painting, too! I painted that." Holbrook pointed eagerly at *Starry Sky*.

Rumolde shook his sleek head, almost as if he were sad.

"I took him in, you see," Rumolde explained to the crowd. "He was alone in the city. Starving. Homeless. I showed him my studio. There he saw *Starry Sky*. Now he seems to imagine he painted it. My servant Grayler will tell you that I painted *Starry Sky* in my studio."

"Yes, indeed," said Grayler, stepping forward.

"No!" cried Holbrook.

He strained to see over the crowd. Where were Margot and the others? Then he noticed that Frick blocked the doorway they had sailed through on the cart.

Holbrook suddenly realized that Enrico and Margot had never actually seen *Starry Sky*, only *Desert Sunset*. There was no one in the city who could say for sure that *Starry Sky* was his!

"It is well known that Rumolde has been working on his art for years," said Corvus.

Wartsnall, who stood nearby, nodded. So did many of the other animals.

Holbrook looked at Rumolde. So rich and important. A famous patron of the arts. His voice was so soothing and reasonable, his smile so friendly. Perhaps he would even convince Margot and Enrico and the others that they had been mistaken about the night before!

"And after all my kindness, he accuses me of wanting to eat him and others!" Rumolde's voice began to rise. "He is delusional! Mad!"

Holbrook noticed that Grayler and Squeak were moving toward him.

"He must be put away," cried Rumolde above a growing tide of confused squawks and squeaks and barks. "For his own good!"

Grayler clutched Holbrook's arm, his grip like iron.

"Come, lizard," he muttered under his breath.

Squeak grabbed his other arm.

"No!" cried Holbrook. He squirmed wildly to break free.

"He's frothing at the mouth!" gasped the Duchess of Woof.

The animals nearest to him drew back. The word "rabid" shuddered through the crowd amid cries of horror and alarm.

"Rabid!" roared Rumolde. This was the ultimate

triumph! Not even someone as famous as Enrico could save Holbrook if the crowd feared rabies.

Suddenly, cutting through the noise came a small cooing voice. "Make way for the poor. Make way for the poor."

One Leg hobbled through the crowd, carefully keeping his second leg out of sight so he might look as pathetic as possible. Behind him came Lone Eye and Scabs. They tottered up to Wartsnall and the others carrying Holbrook's painting of One Leg.

"What's this?" asked the hedgehog.

"Get the lizard out of here!" cried Rumolde, gesturing angrily at Squeak and Grayler.

But the pigeons blocked their path.

"We brought this painting," announced One Leg, "to enter in the Exhibition."

Holbrook remembered how he'd told the pigeons to pretend his painting was theirs. But now he needed the animals to see that he was the artist, not the pigeons!

"That's another of my paintings," he said quickly.

Wartsnall and Cawfield glanced at each other.

Holbrook felt hot. He *did* sound crazy—claiming yet another painting as his.

And Rumolde knew it. His eyes gleamed. "What did I tell you!" the mink declared. "He probably wants credit for every entry in the Exhibition. He probably imagines that he, not Enrico, sang the opera. He probably imagines that Maurice's feast was his idea. He is desperate to be considered a real artist. He imagines that he, not Margot Frogtayne, danced!"

The animals in the crowd began to laugh.

"No, that's not true—" Holbrook tried to speak above the laughter. But no one was listening. All eyes were now on Wartsnall, who turned to the pigeons and asked, "Did you or the lizard do this painting?"

Scabs looked away, as she always did, and Holbrook remembered with a sinking heart how the pigeons never really answered anything. But then she raised her head, stared right at Wartsnall, and said clearly, "Holbrook did it."

"Yes," said Lone Eye firmly. "I watched him do it myself."

And One Leg said, "He saw that I was the King of Pigeons, disguised, banished from my kingdom. I don't remember, but Holbrook knew. Clearly, he is a great artist."

"The pigeons are lying," Rumolde said, brushing a paw over his golden streak. "Look at them. Smelly beggars!"

"Well, that one's his, too," said One Leg nodding at *Starry Sky.* "We saw it in his backpack when he first came to town. It's not as nice as the portrait of me, of course, but . . ."

Holbrook remembered the pigeons' greedy curiosity about his pack and its contents that first day in town.

Now all the animals turned back to Rumolde.

The mink did not look so calm and sleek. He

glanced at Squeak and Grayler, who drew close to him. A solid front.

"They're lying!" Rumolde declared, facing the crowd. "Who can you believe? Nobodies or me!"

"Nobodies!" Enrico's voice boomed over the throng, and he pushed his way through all the creatures clustered around Holbrook. "Rumolde is the one who lies!"

"He planned to slaughter us!" trumpeted Miss Gosling, waddling up behind him.

"For our great talent," she added, modestly.

"I don't know how they got by me, boss," said Frick, hurrying up to Rumolde. "The door was locked and everything."

"You forgot the servant's entrance, my dear sir," exclaimed Homarus, clicking his claw at Frick and looking quite pleased with himself. "That's where snobbery will get you!"

"Count Rumolde is a fraud," Margot said. "*And* a cannibal."

And there was no doubting her quiet firmness.

Rumolde turned and snatched up *Starry Sky*.

"*I* did it!" he shouted. "*I'm* the one!"

He charged for the door, battering at the crowd with the painting.

Holbrook leapt for him, grabbed an ankle, and hung on.

"Get your filthy mitts off me!" Rumolde snarled. "Don't you know who I am? I am the greatest artist in the world!"

He lunged forward, but Holbrook flung out his tail, tripping him. *Starry Sky* flew from his hands and skittered across the floor. The mink dove for it. "I did it!" he cried.

But before he could reach it, he was snatched by the scruff of the neck by a giant German shepherd.

"*No!*" Rumolde shrieked. He twisted in the paws of the police dog. "I am the greatest! Me! Me!"

Cawfield gazed at him with sad eyes. "I am afraid, count, that *you* are the one who is mad."

"And there's more proof," cried Holbrook. "In the basement of the Mordred Arms is a factory—a sweat-shop for artists who work like prisoners. I'll show you!"

"Maurice!" cried Rumolde. "Grayler! Squeak! Stop him!"

But his servants had vanished into the crowd.

"Take him away," said Wartsnall.

As the dog marched Rumolde out, the mink made one last desperate lunge at *Starry Sky*. "Mine!" he cried slashing at it with his sharp claws. "Mine!"

And one claw did reach the canvas, scratching across the dark blue sky. But to everyone's astonishment, the small white streak it left looked like a shooting star across the heavens. The final perfect touch!

Even Holbrook knew that it added something to the painting, but Rumolde wasn't around to see it. The police dog had carted him off like a rotten bone.

"We must free the artists!" cried Holbrook.

And the crowd turned as one and surged out the door and up the street to the Mordred Arms.

"Here, now! What's going on!" cried the cockatoo, but no one paid him any attention. With Holbrook in the lead, they swarmed down the stairs to the basement.

"Free them! Free them! Free them!" the crowd chanted.

Ironlung charged out the door of the workroom with an angry howl, took one look at the crowd, turned, and ran. All the other guards tore off behind him, their claws clattering desperately on the cement.

Holbrook burst through the doorway into the workroom.

"You're free!" he cried, running over to Maxwell.

Maxwell looked up from his kittens. The mouse looked up from her meadows. The mole looked up from his ocean waves. All the animals looked up wearily from their pink roses and mountain lakes and spring leaves. It took a moment, and then, with a roar, they tossed their paintbrushes into the air.

28

"It is with supreme pleasure that I announce the winners of the Golden City Artiste Exhibition Extraordinaire."

The head judge, Mr. L'Owl, stood at the microphone on a stage in the Exhibition Hall. All around Holbrook, animals of every sort murmured and jostled each other excitedly.

After freeing the artists, they had all returned to the Exhibition Hall. At last, the performances began. Ms. Swanson and Margot and many other ballerinas danced their hearts out. Great operatic voices boomed through the hall.

Holbrook and Maxwell strolled among the paintings. There were so many wonderful ones. All so different. Some small. Some big. Some with paint as thick as a finger, some with paints so thin, they looked like colored water. There were trees and ocean waves, even a few kittens, but they were trees and ocean waves and kittens as only that one creature saw them. No one else would ever paint a kitten or a tree in quite the same way, because they all came from the thing inside, which was different and special for each creature.

And when they were especially good, Holbrook felt he saw the trees and ocean waves and all the other things of the world in a special way, too.

There was a picture by Andy Wartsnall with a real can of dog food stuck in it. Maxwell stared at it, shaking his head. "Imagine that," he said. "I think I'll still paint kittens. But I'm getting lots of ideas."

Holbrook smiled and patted the gentle pug on the back.

"I suppose in art there are really no winners or losers," Mr. L'Owl continued at the microphone, slowly turning his head and blinking his large yellow eyes.

"Open the envelopes," honked Miss Gosling under her breath. "Tell us later there are no winners."

Perhaps the owl heard her, because he suddenly stopped and cleared his throat. "Well, that's enough talk. The envelopes, please."

And with a quick slice of his talon, he opened the first envelope.

"In Ballet . . ."

Margot held herself high and tried to look uninterested.

". . . Mademoiselle Margot Frogtayne."

The leap she made to the stage was her finest of the evening.

★★

And so it went.

Enrico won in Opera. Even Homarus won an award for Art Criticism. They were all up on the stage holding their awards while the crowd clapped and threw flowers.

And then Mr. L'Owl opened the envelope for First Place in Painting. "And the winner is . . ."

Holbrook thought he might stop breathing. His pulse pounded against his throat. What if he should win? It wasn't possible, but still, what if—

"Corvus Cawfield!"

The shining black crow stepped forward. Holbrook knew it had been crazy to imagine he would win. It was just that after all those years of teasing and laughing in the desert, he had hoped so much that the world would see he was a real artist.

Holbrook pushed desperately against the packed animals. He had to get out of there. Suddenly, he missed his desert home with all his heart.

"This year, we also have a special award," the owl continued, holding up a wing to quiet the crowd. "A special judges' award for the Most Promising Newcomer.

"It's Holbrook the lizard! Where is Holbrook?"

"Uh?"

They were calling his name. Maxwell pushed him toward the stage.

"I am so proud!" cried Margot. "Holbrook, you have won the newcomer award! You are to join the World Tour along with the rest of us!"

Someone thrust a golden medal into his hands, and Margot flung her arms around him and planted a kiss on his cheek.

Holbrook blushed the color of a desert sunset.

29

The shiny red car eased off the paved road and jounced down a rutted dirt track, stopping not far from Irving's General Store and Desert Diner.

The animals of Rattler's Bend peered uneasily from their dwellings. What was a car doing here?

Irving limped to the door of his store.

The car doors opened. To everyone's astonishment, out hopped a beautiful frog . . . and Holbrook!

The frog took Holbrook's arm and gave it a happy squeeze.

Holbrook glanced around. Even though he'd only been gone a few weeks, he'd expected Rattler's Bend to be different. But it looked just the same.

He spotted Irving peering out at him.

"Hey," he cried and hurried up to the store. The entire population of Rattler's Bend tumbled out of their homes and followed him.

"I won Most Promising Newcomer at the Exhibition!" he announced before Irving could say a word. "Look." He held up his medal. "And look at this!" He handed Irving a copy of the *Golden City Animal Gazette.*

"That's me!" He pointed to the big picture on the front page of the newspaper.

Margot, Enrico, Corvus Cawfield, and all the other big winners smiled from the front row. You could barely make Holbrook out. He was shoved to the back behind Homarus Cray Lobster, but he was there.

Holbrook noticed Jagger peering at him from behind the door of Irving's.

Irving's jaw seemed to have stopped working, but finally he sputtered out, "Well, imagine that!"

The red-spotted toad grabbed the paper and scanned the story with her bulging eyes. "It says here they're to go on a world tour. They're gonna meet kings and queens and whatnot. The greatest artists in the world and—" The toad stared at Holbrook for a moment, blinking slowly. "Well, *him,* too!"

"I always said he would be famous," insisted Crink. Crank nodded vigorously.

All the animals began to nod and murmur agreement.

"I knew you wouldn't be playing around forever," said the chuckwalla.

A young Gila stared at Holbrook with shining eyes.

Holbrook couldn't believe it! None of them had ever said anything like that. But he just smiled and

reached a hand out to Irving. "I came back to say goodbye," he said. "And to say thank you."

"Why, it was nothing, young fella," announced the chuckwalla. "Rattler's Bend supports its own."

Holbrook grasped Irving's rough fingers. "Thank you," he said.

Irving blinked and mumbled something about "told you so," although it was impossible to know what he thought he had told Holbrook. Finally, he cleared his throat. "Would you like a pickled egg?" he asked.

"No, I just need to pick up a few things, and then I'd better go."

All the creatures turned to look out at the red car and at Margot, who stood demurely beside it.

"Now, that," announced Irving, "is a sight I never thought I'd see."

And it was impossible to say if he meant the car or Margot.

Holbrook quickly introduced her to the dazzled crowd.

"Holbrook has told me so much about his lovely desert home," Margot said, glancing about with her sparkling dark eyes.

Every dusty lizard and toad in Rattler's Bend stood just a little taller, and they followed her into Irving's, hanging on every word.

"I am so thrilled to meet all of Holbrook's cowboy friends," she said.

The animals glanced at each other, but no one

bothered to correct her. The brown chuckwalla even blurted out a "Yes'm, little lady." And walked as though he had spurs on.

Holbrook headed out to his burrow.

He rolled up his paintings and squeezed them into his backpack. He would see if Irving would store them for him. Then he picked up his old paint box and headed back.

Jagger stood uncertainly by the door, watching for him.

"You still got that squiggle painting?" the horned lizard asked.

"They want it for a museum in Golden City," said Holbrook.

"Museum?" said Jagger. "That's pretty fancy."

Holbrook nodded. Even he couldn't quite believe it. "It might even be in a book," he said.

He ran his forepaw over his battered paint box, then suddenly thrust it toward Jagger. "I wanted to give you this."

"Hey, whatja doing?" Jagger jumped back.

"You can use it when you paint. And there're some books, too. Back in my burrow."

"Paint? Who said I wanted to paint anything?" Jagger said, but his fingers closed around the box handle.

Margot stepped gracefully from Irving's.

"We must go, Holbrook. We have to catch zee ship for zee Grand Tour," she said. She turned to wave at all the creatures inside Irving's, who stood watching them with their snouts pressed against the window. Everyone raised a paw to wave back.

"Be sure to write. Folks'll want to know about meeting with royalty and whatnot," said Irving.

Holbrook nodded. He wondered when he would return to Rattler's Bend. Someday, he'd visit with Irving and maybe even eat a pickled egg. He would see Jagger's paintings. He thought they might be pretty interesting. He would stand again beneath the desert sky and gaze up at the stars. So far away and yet, somehow, so near, too.

Jagger thrust out his paw to shake Holbrook's. "Thanks," he blurted, then darted his eyes around angrily, daring anyone to laugh, but only Irving was near. "I won't paint squiggles," he said, but then he swiveled one bright eye toward Holbrook. "But I might paint spots."

And Holbrook thought he saw the flicker of a smile. "Good luck," he said, grinning back. "Maybe I can show you Golden City someday."

And he meant it.

And then he quickly hopped into the waiting car. After all, there was a mighty big world to see.

Some famous artists and their works provided inspiration for my story. I am grateful to them all for their wonderful art. Here are the real people. I bet you can see where they showed up, but a little bit changed, in my story:

VINCENT VAN GOGH (1853–1890): Dutch painter known for his unusual style. One of his most famous paintings is a swirling night sky called *Starry Night*. In his life he sold only a few paintings, but his pictures now sell for many millions of dollars and are among the most loved works of art in the world. You can see *Starry Night* at the Museum of Modern Art in New York.

MARGOT FONTEYN (1919–1991): One of the most famous ballerinas ever, her dancing was considered elegant yet passionate. Margot Fonteyn was from England, but just because I like the way it sounds, I made my character, Margot Frogtayne, speak as if she's French.

ENRICO CARUSO (1873–1921): Italian singer. One of the most renowned tenors in opera history, he gave hundreds of peformances and made many recordings, including the aria *"E lucevan le stelle,"* from the opera *Tosca* (mentioned below).

GIACOMO PUCCINI (1858–1924): Italian composer of operas, including *Tosca,* in which the hero is imprisoned. While awaiting his execution, the hero sings about the shimmering stars and the loss of life and his dreams of love.

T. S. ELIOT (1888–1965): Born in America, but later a British citizen, Eliot was a poet and literary critic who wrote a poem called "The Love Song of J. Alfred Prufrock." In this poem are several famous phrases, including the line: "I have measured out my life with coffee spoons."

ANDY WARHOL (1928–1987): An American artist whose work was controversial because he did things like paint images of Campbell soup cans over and over. Some people said his work wasn't art because it wasn't about serious ideas and images, but other people said it showed that the images of ordinary life—like the labels on soup cans—were important.

ROD MCKUEN (1933–): A best-selling American poet. At one time, he was perhaps the most popular poet in the United States. One of his books was called *Stanyan Street and Other Sorrows.*

DASHIELL HAMMETT (1894–1961): An American author who wrote detective stories, many set in San Francisco, that touched on the dark side of city life. One of his best-known novels was *The Maltese Falcon,* later made into a movie.